Daggers and Disguises

A Magical Mystery from the Enchanted Antique Shop

CIELLE KENNER

Dressed to Thrill

Welcome to Enchanted Springs, where ghosts are friendly, magic is real, and time is anything but linear.

Marley Montgomery, proprietor of the Enchanted Antique Shop, is ready for a spellbinding Halloween in her magical small town. But when a midnight matinee at the Parthenon Theater turns deadly, Marley finds herself entangled in a mystery worthy of the silver screen.

Time literally stands still as Marley and her eclectic ensemble—from both sides of the veil—sift through secrets, lies, and shocking betrayals.

Will Marley unmask the killer before the final curtain call? Or will this Halloween mystery remain cloaked in darkness forever?

Step into the enchantment of Halloween in a small town where magic and mystery go hand in hand.

Bonus Content

Get maps, character profiles, and free bonus content at ciellekenner.com.

Claim your copy of *Death and Doughnuts*, a free mini mystery from the Enchanted Oven bakery! bit.ly/deathanddoughnuts

Copyright Notice

Cast of Characters

The Regulars

MARLEY MONTGOMERY: Proprietor of the Enchanted Antique Shop, time traveler, and ghost whisperer. Also a professional photographer.

CLARA MONTGOMERY: Marley's grandmother, owner of the Enchanted Oven bakery, and head of the magical Council of Guardians.

ELEANOR SOMERVILLE: Clara's best friend, Marley's mentor, retired proprietor of the Enchanted Antique Shop.

SADIE ARRAGON: Marley's best friend. History professor by day, spellcaster by night, and associate proprietor of the Enchanted Antique Shop.

VIOLET SERRANO: The vivacious spirit of a 1920s flapper era, now living her best Afterlife at the Enchanted Antique Shop.

JACK EDGEWOOD: The vampire detective with a sharp wit and even sharper senses.

CIELLE KENNER

Guest Stars

LARRY LINWOOD: President of the Parthenon Theater's board of directors.
JOANNA ELLIOTT: Director of the Parthenon Theater.
FRANCES BUTNER: Treasurer of the Parthenon Theater.
ROBERT HARPER: Attorney and Parthenon Theater volunteer.

Contents

CHAPTER 1

Monsters on Main Street

THE SCENT OF PUMPKIN spice and mischief filled the air, and my grandmother's bakery was bustling.

Normally, the Enchanted Oven bakeshop looked like a cozy country kitchen. Tonight, however, she had transformed it into a sleek, monochrome masterpiece—perfect for Halloween. Gone were the checkered tablecloths and cheerful floral curtains. Now, the theme was an elegant, vintage noir décor—everything in black and white.

Outside, the bakery's window display featured oversized white pumpkins nestled among glossy black ribbons and twinkling fairy lights. They cast an enchanting glow over a hand-painted sign that read, "Welcome, Monsters on Main."

Black velvet curtains draped the windows, giving the space a shadowy, upscale speakeasy vibe. Silver candelabras topped with flickering candles added a touch of mystery, while crystal vases filled with pale baby's breath sat on each café table. Even the bakery's signature pastel shelves had been charmed with magic, adopting the midnight motif for the night. The jars of candy

1

and baked goods within seemed to glow against their stark surroundings, as if they were part of a black-and-white photograph, brought to life.

Grandma Clara flitted about in a chic black dress, her pearl necklace gleaming under the soft glow of hanging lamps draped with sheer, web-like fabric. A large, paper crescent moon hung above the counter, its surface dusted with iridescent glitter to mimic the glow of moonlight—a nod to tonight's midnight movie showing.

"The stars of the show," she said with a wink, gesturing to her artfully arranged display of Halloween treats: charcoal-black macarons with white chocolate filling, sugar cookies dusted in edible silver glitter, and cupcakes crowned with dark chocolate ganache and candied violets.

I stood by her side, handing out treats and trying not to get too distracted by the parade of costumes passing by the bakery windows. Main Street had come alive for "Monsters on Main," our town's annual Halloween festival. Costumed families paraded down the cobblestone sidewalks, stopping at each local business to trick-or-treat. Lively, hand-carved jack-o'-lanterns grinned in shop windows, while bundles of yellow and orange mums lined the walkways, their blossoms glowing under the soft streetlights.

I caught a glimpse of myself in the bakery's glass door. My hair, a wild mane of auburn curls, was already rebelling against the vintage-style pin I'd tried to secure it with. Before I could smooth it down, Grandma Clara appeared at my side, her hands quick and efficient as she attempted to tame the chaos atop my head.

"Hold still, pumpkin," she murmured, deftly twisting a particularly unruly curl back into place. "You look just like me when I was your age—stubborn curls and all." She stepped back, a soft smile tugging at her lips.

"Oh, really? I thought you were the picture of elegance back then," I teased, turning to face her.

She laughed, a sound like the chime of a vintage clock, and adjusted the collar of my black-and-white dress. "Elegance takes practice, darling. And a lot of bobby pins." Her eyes crinkled at the corners, a sparkle of nostalgia shining through. "You should've seen me back in my youth. I was always fighting with my curls, just like you. It's a Montgomery trait. Passed down through generations."

I glanced at her, admiring how effortlessly she pulled off her look tonight. Her auburn hair, a shade darker than mine, was swept into a neat twist, with soft curls framing her face. A string of pearls hugged her neck, a classic contrast to the sleek black dress she wore. She always made everything seem so easy, so timeless.

"Well, at least one of us mastered it," I said, adjusting the strap of my purse. "And here I thought I'd inherited only your stubbornness."

Her green eyes twinkled as she gave me a playful nudge. "Oh, you got that too. Trust me. But it'll serve you well, especially in this town." She paused, studying me for a moment. "You really do look just like me, you know—just with a bit more sass."

I grinned, a warm surge of pride spreading through me. "I'll take that as a compliment."

3

"It is," she said, smoothing a stray lock of her own hair back into place. "Now, let's get these cupcakes out before we face a monster insurrection."

The bakery smelled heavenly—a blend of warm vanilla, cinnamon, and dark cocoa drifting through the air, mingling with the sharper scent of freshly brewed coffee. Soft jazz wafted from hidden speakers, adding to the sultry, timeless ambiance. From 5 to 7 p.m., it was all about the kids—candy buckets, parades, and the thrill of a costume contest judged by none other than the mayor himself.

Clara nudged me as I handed a cookie to a child dressed as a vampire. "Look at all the little monsters, Marley. This is my favorite time of year."

"Mine too," I said, scanning the crowd outside. I spotted a group of teenagers in their best slasher-film costumes and a couple of adults dressed as mummies. "It's like everyone gets to be their truest self, at least for one night."

She chuckled, her eyes twinkling. "That's the magic of Halloween, isn't it?"

I nodded, turning my attention back to a little girl dressed as a fairy princess. "What's your favorite Halloween treat?"

She shyly pointed to the frosted cupcakes. I handed one over with a smile. "Good choice!"

As the clock neared eight, a different energy settled over the town. Shopkeepers switched out bowls of candy for thermoses of mulled cider, and the event shifted into adult territory. Out came the more elaborate costumes—creatures of the night, masked phantoms, and vintage Hollywood stars. The late-night movie marathon awaited, but for now, the streets were filled with laughter, light, and just a touch of the supernatural.

I never thought I'd return to my hometown, much less end up running the Enchanted Antique Shop. But life has a way of surprising you, especially when you hit your Saturn return—a cosmic curveball that flips everything upside down. That's when I discovered my own magic, just like my grandmother Clara and the rest of the local magical community here in Enchanted Springs. Now, I manage the antique shop, which is more than just a quaint storefront; it's a hidden gateway to the past, nestled right across the street from my grandma's bakery.

When I'm not selling relics from bygone eras, I'm usually knee-deep in a mystery involving the town's colorful—and occasionally ghostly—residents. You see, I can see spirits, thanks to my magical abilities. And trust me, history in this town isn't just sitting around collecting dust. It's alive, whispering secrets from every shadowy corner.

Trouble has a way of finding me, though. Maybe it's the shop's mysterious aura, or maybe it's just Enchanted Springs itself. Either way, things get complicated fast. And tonight, with Halloween and the "Monsters on Main" festival in full swing, I had a feeling things were about to get a lot more interesting.

CHAPTER 2

Dressed to Thrill

A S THE CHILDREN'S PORTION of the festivities wound down, the bakery settled into a more relaxed hum. The crowd thinned, and for a moment, there was a quiet lull. Then the door creaked open, and in swept Violet Serrano, the ghost of a 1920s flapper, dressed up in a twist on her usual look.

"Happy Halloween, kittens!" she trilled, gliding across the floor as though she owned the place. Tonight, she had transformed herself into an exaggerated version of a ghost, fully embracing her ethereal status. Her signature drop-waist black dress with beads and fringe swayed with every step, catching the dim light of the bakery. But it was her face that stole the show. She had powdered it a stark white, her eyes heavily lined in smoky circles, and her lips painted a rich blood-red. Violet had gone for drama, looking every inch the ghostly flapper come to haunt the living.

I caught sight of Clara's face and had to stifle a laugh at the amusement dancing in her eyes. Only Violet, dead for a hundred years, would choose a ghost costume for Halloween.

"Hi Violet," I called, feigning innocence. "It's getting late. When do you plan to change into your costume?"

She tilted her chin up with a sly smile, her eyes sparkling with mischief. "Very funny, doll face." She stuck out her tongue and waggled her fingers at me. "All kidding aside, I make quite the spectral spectacle, don't you think?" She floated past the pastry display like she was on a runway, turning heads with every swish of her beaded dress.

Usually, only a select few with magical sight could see her, but tonight? Oh, tonight, everyone saw Violet. It was Halloween, and the veil between worlds was practically non-existent. To the uninitiated, she was just another reveler in a fantastic costume. But to us, it was a grand joke that she was actually a ghost playing a ghost.

Clara turned from the counter, flour dusting her hands. "Violet, darling, help yourself to the shortbread," she said with a wink. "We've got plenty."

Violet dipped into a graceful curtsy, every movement fluid and dramatic. "Don't mind if I do." She reached for a shortbread cookie shaped like a crescent moon, lifting it delicately to her lips. A couple of customers nearby watched, wide-eyed, completely entranced by her theatrical presence. They had no idea they were in the company of an actual ghost. To them, she was just an incredibly convincing actress.

"You do make quite the entrance," Clara remarked, handing her another cookie. "Happy Halloween, Violet."

Violet accepted it with a flourish. "Ah, heaven!" she sighed, taking a dainty bite. "The one night I get to indulge, and no one bats an eye." She cast a sly glance around the bakery, her eyes gleaming beneath the dark makeup. "Tell me, do I look hauntingly fabulous?"

The room filled with polite laughter, and a few confused murmurs rippled through the crowd. Most assumed she was a guest in costume—albeit a very dedicated one.

"You look incredible!" someone called from the back. Violet gave a theatrical bow, the beads on her dress clinking like tiny wind chimes.

"Why, thank you, darling!" she replied, spinning on her heel. The beads on her dress caught the candlelight, casting tiny stars across the bakery walls. "A little extra haunting never hurt, hmm?" She turned and winked at me, her face alight with glee.

I couldn't help but grin at her antics, marveling at the irony of a real ghost playing pretend. "You nailed it, Violet. You're the life of the party."

"Well, I try," she said airily, brushing off an imaginary speck of dust from her dress. "One must keep up appearances, after all."

CHAPTER 3

Halloween Happenings

As GRAM AND I wiped down the counters and turned off the lights, I couldn't help but glance out the window at the mingling crowd. Monsters and ghouls laughed and shared candy like old friends, their costumes glowing under the orange streetlights.

But if you looked closely, past the flickering jack-o'-lanterns and cobweb-draped storefronts, you'd see the true magic of Enchanted Springs. Paranormals walked openly among the costumed revelers, their real forms masquerading as mere dress-up. A towering, horned figure, his skin the color of polished obsidian, lumbered down the sidewalk, his laughter a deep rumble that shook the air; a real, live ogre, but friendly. Beside him, a delicate woman floated just an inch above the ground, her translucent gown trailing behind her like wisps of mist, her eyes glowing a soft, eerie blue; a will-o'-the-wisp. She stopped for a moment to chat with a group of witches who had gathered on the corner.

Further down the street, a pair of pixies flitted through the air, their wings shimmering with iridescent colors in the dim light.

They darted between costumed children, sprinkling tiny trails of sparkling dust that made the streetlights gleam brighter for a moment before fading away. Most of the passersby didn't seem to notice them at all, assuming them to be clever tricks of light. Only the few who were attuned to the town's magic turned to watch the spectacle with wide eyes and hushed whispers.

Closer to the bakery, I spotted a figure in an elegant cloak lined with silver embroidery, their face hidden beneath a hood that cast shadows over their features. As they stepped into the light, their skin shimmered with a faint, unnatural sheen, betraying their true nature—a fae lord come to join the festivities. A pair of small horns peeked out from under the hood, and when they lifted their head, their eyes glowed with a golden hue that reflected the harvest moon hanging low in the sky.

Beside them, a tall man in an old-fashioned suit stood talking to a group of people in Victorian-era attire. His skin had a slight grayish tint, and his hands bore long, curved fingernails. He tipped his hat politely as he nodded to something one of his companions said, revealing teeth that were just a bit too sharp to be human. A vampire, no doubt, relishing the chance to walk among mortals without needing to hide his true nature.

I caught a glimpse of a small, shadowy creature slinking along the edge of the square, its eyes glowing a vivid yellow as it moved. It had the form of a cat, but its tail was unnaturally long, curling and twisting like a serpent as it prowled through the throng. A kitsune, I realized, disguised for the evening in its feline form.

There, beneath a lamppost, a ghostly woman in a Victorian gown hovered, her expression serene as she watched the celebrations unfold. Wisps of fog curled around her feet, making her appear as if she'd stepped straight out of a bygone era. People walked right through her without noticing, too engrossed in their own merriment to sense the spectral presence among them.

And then, in a darkened doorway, I spotted a hulking figure cloaked in black, his eyes glowing crimson in the darkness. A reaper. His skeletal fingers clutched a silver dagger-shaped pendant that glinted ominously under the streetlights. I shivered, hoping he wasn't here for a reason. With any luck, he was just a man in a costume, another part of the macabre tapestry that wove the town together on Halloween.

As usual, there were a few ghosts wandering past, as well. Not like Violet, who practically shimmered with personality, but more subdued, everyday specters of Enchanted Springs' past. There was Phil McKinley, the town's favorite former mailman, striding down the street with his old leather satchel slung over one shoulder. His uniform buttons gleamed in the streetlights as he tipped his hat to passersby, whistling a tune that only I seemed to hear. To him, it was just another day on his route, blissfully unaware that the world had changed around him.

Across the street, Mrs. Beatrice O'Malley hovered near the entrance of the flower shop, her ghostly form wrapped in a dark shawl. She adjusted her round spectacles and peered through the window, a bemused smile curling at her lips as if marveling at how times had changed. Her spirit always lingered around this spot, where her husband's cigar shop once stood. Tonight, though, she seemed more vibrant, her edges clearer than usual, as if the thinning of the veil had breathed a bit of life back into her.

At the corner, I noticed a young soldier in a World War II uniform, a bit lost in the shuffle. His cap was tipped at an angle, and he looked around as if searching for someone in the crowd. I recognized him instantly—Peter Callahan, who'd never made it back from the war. He'd been known to haunt the square on quiet nights, but tonight, surrounded by the hubbub of costumed townsfolk, he seemed less like a lost soul and more like just another participant in the evening's revelry. A woman dressed as Rosie the Riveter walked right through him, completely unaware of the spectral encounter.

The real magic of Halloween in Enchanted Springs wasn't in the decorations or even the costumes—it was in the blending of worlds, the way the supernatural could step into the light for one night, mingling with the mundane. Tonight, the monsters on Main Street weren't confined to the realm of imagination. They were real, and they were out to play.

"You know," I mused, more to myself than anyone else, "Halloween really is the one night when everything and everyone isn't quite what it seems."

Grandma Clara paused in the middle of stacking the last of the cookie trays. She looked up, her eyes thoughtful, reflecting the glimmer of candlelight from the centerpiece candelabra. "Or maybe," she said gently, "it's the one night when we get to see things as they truly are."

I smiled at that, knowing there was truth in her words. Halloween in Enchanted Springs wasn't just about trick-or-treaters or costumes. It was the joining of two worlds, where the veil between the seen and unseen grew thin, allowing magic to breathe freely.

I glanced at the clock on the far wall, its hands ticking closer to eight. The children's portion of the festival was winding down, which meant it was almost time for the grown-ups to take over. And for us, that meant heading off to the Parthenon Theater for the late-night showing of *Daggers and Disguises*.

I turned to Gram, who was now wiping her hands on her apron, and said, "Looks like we're about ready to close up shop."

She nodded, casting a glance out at the bustling street, now filling with adults in more elaborate costumes. "It's going to be quite the night. Do you have everything you need for the movie?"

"Got the tickets." I patted the phone in my pocket. "Are you and Eleanor still planning on going?"

"Oh, absolutely," Gram replied with a grin, her eyes twinkling with mischief. "You know how much Eleanor and I love a good classic mystery."

Eleanor Somerville, my grandmother's best friend and former proprietor of the Enchanted Antique Shop, had been my mentor and guide since I returned to Enchanted Springs. She'd passed the guardianship of her shop—and its secrets—on to me. More importantly, she was the one who'd first taught me about the time portal hidden in the back room.

As if on cue, Violet floated over, her eyes gleaming. "It'll be like stepping back in time. I haven't been to a proper picture show since the 'twenties."

I stifled a laugh. "Leave it to you, Violet, to turn a movie night into a trip down memory lane."

With that, we began shutting down the bakery, anticipation buzzing in the air. Outside, the Monsters on Main event continued in full swing.

Clara moved to the door and flipped the sign to "Closed," her hand lingering on the glass pane for a moment as she surveyed the scene outside.

"Well, that was fun," she said, turning back to me with a smile. "Ready for part two?"

15

"Absolutely," I replied, already feeling a flutter of excitement in my stomach. The night was young, and *Daggers and Disguises* awaited us at the Parthenon Theater.

Clara straightened a stack of napkins on the counter, her eyes gleaming. "Have you ever been to a midnight matinee, Marley?" she asked, her grin rivaling that of a jack-o'-lantern.

I chuckled, brushing a stray curl behind my ear. "Not since college, Gram. I'm usually in bed long before midnight these days."

"Oh, but this is different!" She waved a flour-dusted hand in the air, dismissing my practicalities with a flourish. "It's *Daggers and Disguises*! A true noir classic packed with intrigue, deception, and a twist that'll leave you speechless. And tonight, it's showing in its original, uncut version!" Her eyes sparkled as she picked up a crescent moon cookie, brandishing it like a prop. "Eleanor and I used to watch it in the theater when we were your age. Trust me, there's nothing like seeing it on the big screen. The suspense, the drama—oh, it gives me chills just thinking about it!"

I chuckled, wiping my hands on my apron. "You and Eleanor sound more excited than the kids trick-or-treating outside."

Clara laughed, a warm, melodic sound that filled the room. "Why shouldn't we be? It's Halloween! And besides, this movie is a masterpiece. You're in for a treat, mark my words."

Clara turned from the display, adjusting her pearl necklace. "I'd go even if I didn't care for the film. I need to be present for all the night's events. It's my duty as head of the Council of Guardians. Someone has to make sure everything stays safe and orderly, especially when the veil is this thin."

"Right," I replied, glancing outside where a vampire couple—real vampires, mind you—strolled by hand in hand. "It's quite the balancing act."

The Council of Guardians was the governing body for Enchanted Springs' paranormal community. They ensured that magic, spirits, and all things supernatural flowed smoothly and stayed hidden when necessary. Grandma Clara, as head of the Council, was both respected and feared—a position she managed with a mix of grace, grit, and more than a dash of humor.

She turned back to me, her expression one of calm determination. "Halloween is our biggest test every year. The council has to ensure the boundaries stay intact while allowing our community the freedom to enjoy themselves. It's like herding cats, really."

"Well," I said, smirking as I untied my apron, "it's a good thing you're great at herding."

I glanced at the clock on the bakery wall, noting the time. "I should head out, Gram. I'll swing by Sadie's place to pick her up, and we'll meet you and Eleanor at the theater."

Grandma Clara nodded, her eyes still sparkling with excitement. "Sounds like a plan. Don't keep her waiting; you know how Sadie gets when there's Halloween fun to be had."

I grinned, reaching for my sweater. "Oh, I know. She's probably been ready for hours."

"Then go on, dear," Clara said, giving me a gentle pat on the shoulder. "Tonight's a night for surprises. Let's enjoy every minute of it."

With a final glance at the window, where costumed figures swirled in the glow of streetlights, I stepped out into the crisp Halloween night. Sadie and the Parthenon awaited, and I had a feeling this midnight matinee would be one to remember.

CHAPTER 4

Trick or Treat

I LAUGHED, GRABBING MY sweater and waving goodbye to the bakery's cozy warmth. Stepping outside, I inhaled the crisp autumn air, rich with a hint of wood smoke.

As I stepped outside, I was greeted by a crispness that was rare for Central Florida this time of year. The air carried the faint scent of rain mixed with the earthy aroma of damp leaves, a promise of fall that we Floridians grasped at whenever the temperature dipped below seventy degrees. It wasn't cold, but it was cool enough to warrant my sweater—a soft, cable-knit number I wore more for the thrill of pretending it was finally autumn than for warmth.

Sadie's house was only a few blocks away, so I decided to walk, soaking up the Halloween magic that filled the town.

As I reached the more residential neighborhoods, glowing jack-o'-lanterns lined the street, their toothy grins flickering against the twilight. Costumed children skipped past, their voices rising in gleeful anticipation as they darted from door to door.

I took a deep breath, letting the fresh, slightly salty breeze from the coast fill my lungs. Above, the sky stretched out like a canvas of indigo velvet, each star etched sharply against its surface. The constellations twinkled with a magical clarity I'd only ever noticed over Enchanted Springs, their brilliance magnified as if the universe had decided tonight was worth showing off a little.

As I made my way toward Sadie's house, a sudden flash caught my eye. I stopped, staring up at a shooting star as it arced gracefully across the sky, leaving behind a silver trail that shimmered for a breathless second. Good fortune or a bad omen? On a night like this, when the veil between worlds was so thin, it was anyone's guess.

I wrapped the sweater more snugly around myself, savoring the coolness that hinted at the mysteries yet to unfold.

A familiar presence brushed against my leg. I glanced down to see Twila, the spectral Siamese kitten who frequented the antique shop, trotting alongside me. Her translucent fur shimmered like moonlight, and her golden eyes glowed with an almost mischievous light. "Well, hello there," I murmured, smiling. "Decided to keep me company?" Twila blinked lazily, her ethereal gaze reflecting the jack-o'-lanterns' fiery glow.

The courthouse clock tolled faintly as we walked, adding a hauntingly charming soundtrack to the evening. Sadie's bungalow came into view, nestled between two towering raintree trees, their leaves a brilliant mix of yellow and gold. Sadie had gone all out with the decorations—her porch adorned with garlands of corn husks and softly glowing pumpkins. An array of whimsical lawn ornaments lined the cobblestone path: black cats, friendly ghosts, and a cheerful witch's hat perched jauntily on a scarecrow.

Sadie Arragon had an eye for aesthetics, but then, she had an eye for everything. She brought both glamour and gravitas to every aspect of her life.

By day, she was a history professor at Magnolia University—the same school where my parents were professors, even though they were currently on sabbatical.

She was also the most talented spellcaster of our generation, a gift that brought her into the Enchanted Antique Shop as an associate proprietor.

Sadie was my ride-or-die, the Thelma to my Louise—only with more spellbooks and fewer car chases. She hailed from Salem, bringing with her a wealth of magical knowledge, which she now shared with me as we navigated the quirky, sometimes baffling traditions of Enchanted Springs. In a lot of ways, our friendship mirrored the lifelong bond between my grandmother Clara and her best friend Eleanor. And just like them, Sadie and I were learning the ins and outs of this magical community together.

I couldn't help but marvel at how she always managed to bring a touch of magic into the mundane—whether it was enchanting her porch for Halloween or making historical lectures at Magnolia sound like epic tales.

Twila leapt onto the porch railing and turned to face me, her tail curling around her paws as if to say, "What are you waiting for?" I chuckled at the little ghost kitten and climbed the steps, just as the front door swung open.

Sadie stood there in her vintage Halloween apron, holding a tray of candy and looking every bit like a model out of a fashion magazine. Her platinum French bob framed her heart-shaped face perfectly, and her piercing blue eyes sparkled with excitement. "Perfect timing, Marley! You can help me with the trick-or-treaters for a bit before we head to the theater."

I stepped inside, immediately enveloped by the warm scents of cinnamon and cloves. The house was its usual charming self, dressed up for Halloween with garlands of dried flowers, antique lanterns casting flickering shadows, and an old-fashioned phonograph playing crackly Halloween tunes. Sadie had the gift of making history come alive—not just as a professor, but in every little detail of her life.

"You brought a guest." She toward Twila, who had followed me inside and now sat at the foot of the stairs, her eyes gleaming mischievously.

"Seems she's ready for some trick-or-treating herself," I quipped, setting down my coat. It was a comfort knowing that, despite Sadie's ethereal beauty and effortless sophistication, she had the same soft spot for stray spirits as I did.

Sadie laughed, her voice rich and melodic. "Take this to the front door. I hear another group coming now." She handed me a tray piled high with homemade candies, each one wrapped in festive paper.

Almost on cue, the sound of giggles and footsteps approached from outside. I opened the door to reveal a group of costumed kids standing on the porch steps: a mini Dracula, a sparkling fairy, and a pirate with an oversized hat. Twila perked up, watching them with keen interest.

"Trick or treat!" they chorused.

"Well, aren't you all a frightful bunch!" I said, holding out the tray. The kids eagerly grabbed their candies, eyes wide as they noticed Twila's ghostly form glowing faintly.

"Is that a real cat?" the fairy asked, eyes as round as saucers.

"In a way," I replied, grinning.

As I helped Sadie pass out candy, I couldn't help but glance toward the sidewalk, where clusters of parents gathered to keep a watchful eye on their costumed kids. Some of them stood under the glow of the streetlights, chatting and laughing as they sipped from steaming mugs of spiced cider or cocoa. The air buzzed with excitement and a hint of mischief—the perfect energy for Halloween.

But as I looked closer, I noticed that not all the parents were quite what they seemed. There, leaning casually against a lamp-post, was a tall figure with a fedora pulled low over his eyes, a faint glimmer of silver at his collar hinting at the charms woven into his clothing to conceal his identity. A pair of elegant women stood nearby, their flawless, porcelain skin glowing under the lamp-light as they whispered to one another, their laughter carrying a melodic, almost hypnotic quality. A dryad, I realized, her long hair adorned with twigs and autumn leaves that glowed softly, like embers nestled among her dark locks.

And then, my eyes fell on a couple standing a bit farther back. The man, his gaze sharp and calculating, had an aura of quiet power that made the hair on the back of my neck prickle. He stood perfectly still, one hand resting protectively on the shoulder of a young boy dressed as a knight. The boy's mother, a woman with eyes that seemed to glow faintly in the shadows, watched him with a calm that belied a hidden strength. Were they vampires? Witches? In Enchanted Springs, anything was possible, especially on Halloween.

I gave Sadie a nudge and tilted my head toward the parents. "Spotted a few more trick-or-treaters of the other variety."

She followed my gaze, a knowing smile creeping onto her lips. "Looks like even the paranormals can't resist a little Halloween fun," she murmured, handing out candy to a mini Frankenstein who had just bounded up the steps.

"Well, when in Rome," I muttered, grinning as the children rushed away, their bags heavy with sweets and their laughter echoing down the street.

"Rome has nothing on Enchanted Springs," she laughed.

Twila gave a soft, approving purr as the children giggled and scampered off to the next house.

Sadie reached for her sweater, turned off the porch light, and warded her front door. "I think that was most of them. We need to get going before we miss the main event."

I nodded, casting one last glance at her charming bungalow. It was a picture-perfect Halloween scene—the glowing pumpkins, whimsical ornaments, and Twila's spectral form completing the tableau. As we linked arms and stepped off the porch, I couldn't help but think how lucky I was to have Sadie by my side for whatever magical misadventures lay ahead.

"Ready when you are," I said, linking my arm through hers. We stepped out into the bustling Halloween night, Twila padding along behind us, her tail high and proud.

CHAPTER 5

The Wizards Market

THE STREETS OF ENCHANTED Springs buzzed with excitement as we approached the Parthenon Theater.

To our left, the historic courthouse glowed beneath a starlit sky, its copper dome now a weathered green. Above its columned balustrade, the courthouse clock chimed ten haunting rings—a solemn reminder that Halloween night was slipping into its darkest, most mystical hours.

Across the street, Courthouse Square had transformed into the Wizards Market. Lanterns bobbed overhead, casting pools of golden light. Everything had an unmistakable shimmer, as though the entire square were caught in a spell.

The square was a riot of sapphire blues, emerald greens, and ruby reds as pop-up tents lined the cobblestone paths. Tables overflowed with glittering treasures: polished crystals of every imaginable shade, bundles of sage and lavender wrapped in twine, enchanted broomsticks with carved wooden handles, and daggers encrusted with opalescent gems.

The tiered fountain at the square's center glistened under the moonlight, its waters sparkling with an ethereal glow. My grandmother had once hinted that its magic drifted on the wind, down every street and around every corner, infusing the town with its enchantment.

The Wizards Market was normally a quarterly affair, a midnight event exclusive to the paranormal community, hidden behind a veil of magic. But tonight, for Halloween, the market had thrown open its arms to all of Enchanted Springs. Tonight, the masks were off—metaphorically speaking, that is.

The square teemed with both paranormals and regular townsfolk, who thought it was just another element of the Monsters on Main festivities. Costumed humans marveled at what they thought were props and performances, while real magic swirled around them.

A wave of otherworldly energy hit me, making my skin tingle. The street was filled with paranormals, their forms flickering between human guises and something more ethereal. It was like stepping into a scene from another world, one that I was only just beginning to understand.

A chill ran down my spine, and for a moment, I felt like an outsider. I had grown up surrounded by magic, but seeing it out here, so open, so unguarded, made me feel small. Vulnerable. These creatures had come to witness something momentous. But what did they see when they looked at me? A girl fumbling with her newfound powers, trying to navigate a world that was so much bigger and more complicated than she had ever imagined?

I glanced at Sadie, who was beaming with excitement. How did she do it? How did she remain so composed in the face of all this? I felt a surge of uncertainty, a question gnawing at me:

Did I really belong here, among these beings? Until recently, I'd been an ordinary photographer in Miami. Could I ever truly be part of this world? The thought lodged itself in my chest, a sharp reminder of how far I still had to go.

Around us, vendors hawked their wares with enticing calls. "Bottled moonlight! Harvested under the Hunter's Moon, guaranteed to reveal secrets!" crooned a woman draped in silver-threaded robes. Nearby, a dark-haired man waved a hand over a collection of jeweled amulets. "Protection from curses and prying eyes!" he declared, his voice like velvet over the din.

The scents of the market washed over me: a blend of roasted chestnuts, spiced pumpkin, and honeyed mead. Somewhere nearby, a bell jingled softly, followed by the hooting of a barred owl.

We wandered past a stall filled with glimmering crystals that pulsed faintly as we approached. A witch, her cloak embroidered with silver sigils, smiled at us from behind the table, revealing a flash of fang-like teeth. Beside her, a man leaned casually against a post, his eyes faintly glowing green in the shadows. A group of teenage vampires in emo garb sauntered past, laughing softly at some private joke.

On the bandstand, a full band of skeletons swayed on the stage, their fingers clacking over their instruments with uncanny dexterity. The lead skeleton, tall and dapper, wore a tattered top hat perched at a jaunty angle atop his bleached skull. His bony fingers danced across the keys of a vintage piano, producing a sound that was both lively and eerie—the perfect soundtrack for Halloween.

The guitarist strummed an old acoustic, his skeletal fingers moving with surprising fluidity as the strings hummed with a smoky, bluesy tune. Beside him, the skeleton on the upright bass plucked the thick strings, the deep notes vibrating through the square like a heartbeat.

A drum set sat in the corner, and the skeleton drummer twirled his sticks effortlessly, his skull bobbing along to the rhythm. Every so often, a stray bone would click or clack, adding an extra beat to the song in a way that seemed both accidental and perfectly timed.

Ordinary passersby might have thought the musicians were wearing body suits with skeleton designs, but the paranormals in the crowd knew better. This was literally a skeleton band.

A sudden flourish from the trumpet player made me jump. The skeleton brought the horn to his grinning mouth, and without a hint of lips or lungs, he began to play. The sound was smooth and haunting, an otherworldly wail that sent shivers down my spine. The notes hung in the air like mist, swirling around us, drawing the crowd in closer.

The skeleton band's final note rang out, echoing off the cobblestones. The crowd burst into applause, completely oblivious to the spectral nature of the performers. The drummer gave a cheeky wink—or what would have been a wink if he had eyes—as he tossed his drumsticks into the air, catching them with a rattling flourish.

I noticed a cloaked figure watching from the shadows. It was the same reaper from earlier, still holding a scythe in one hand. His deep black cloak billowed slightly, though the air around him was still. Only his eyes were visible. They glowed a menacing red from within the hood's depths. I froze, my heart stuttering in my chest. The figure turned his head, ever so slightly, as if sensing my stare. For a heartbeat, those red eyes seemed to flash, a knowing glimmer that chilled me to the bone.

Twila took one look, turned tail, and ran off in the other direction.

"What is it?" Sadie whispered, following my line of sight.

"Over there," I muttered, nodding toward the figure. "Do you see him?"

Sadie squinted through the crowd. "The guy in the Grim Reaper costume? Creepy, but then again, it's Halloween."

I forced a shaky laugh. "Yeah, you're probably right." I tried to mask the unease creeping up my spine. "Let's keep moving."

Sadie nodded, and we continued through the market. I glanced around one last time, half-expecting to see the reaper still standing there. But he was gone, melted into the shadows of the market.

We carried on, passing more stalls, each brimming with fantastical objects. A silversmith shaped moonstones into amulets, his hammer tapping rhythmically, creating sparks that shimmered into tiny stars before vanishing into the air. Next to him, a wizened woman draped in violet silk chanted softly over vials of bubbling potions, their colors shifting like the aurora.

Ahead of us, near the fountain, a group of fae gathered, their wings reflecting the lantern light in hues of indigo and emerald. They sang softly in a language that sounded like the wind rustling through autumn leaves. Humans milled about nearby, marveling at what they assumed were dazzling costumes. They had no idea they were standing among the true denizens of magic.

Sadie appeared beside me, holding up a delicate bracelet threaded with what looked like tiny, twinkling stars. "What's that?" I asked, squinting at the shimmering bauble.

"It's a Starlight Bracelet," Sadie explained, her voice tinged with awe. "It's supposed to enhance your intuition, guiding you when you're in the dark—literally and figuratively." She slipped it onto her wrist, and for a brief moment, the stars on the bracelet flared, casting a soft glow across her face.

"Now that looks handy," I admitted. "Especially tonight."

Sadie grinned, holding her wrist out to admire the bracelet. "Exactly. Who knows what we'll be dealing with after the movie? A little extra intuition couldn't hurt."

The stall owner nodded approvingly. "A wise choice. The stars will guide you when paths become unclear. And tonight, of all nights, one should never venture into the unknown without a little light."

Then, I saw her at the next stall over: a woman standing behind a cluttered booth piled high with clocks and watches. She looked entirely out of place amid the more polished vendors. Dirt streaked her face, and twigs jutted out from her wild, tangled hair. Her patchwork cloak hung from her shoulders in layers, worn and frayed as though it had traveled through centuries. The aura around her was ancient, not malevolent, but certainly powerful—like a force of nature that couldn't be tamed.

Sadie nudged me. "Do you recognize her?"

"Nope. I've never seen her before in my life."

The woman caught my eye and beckoned us closer with a crooked finger. "Come, come," she rasped, her voice like the rustling of wind through dry leaves. "You're looking for something, and I've got just the thing here at my 'second-hand' shop."

Ah. A pun. She was selling an the assortment of vintage clocks and watches scattered across her table.

I hesitated, looking over her wares. Among them lay a delicate, old-fashioned pendant watch, gleaming softly against the rough wood. I reached out, picking it up carefully. Its face was smooth, with fine Roman numerals etched into the silver, and it felt warm, almost alive, in my palm.

The woman smiled, revealing slightly crooked teeth. "That one's special," she murmured. "A timekeeper's charm. Enhances the spells that twist and bend the flow of time. Could come in handy tonight, don't you think?"

A chill ran down my spine. How could she possibly know? I looked at Sadie, who was already admiring a gold pendant watch with two clock faces on it. "Look at this," Sadie said, eyes wide. "Two clocks, side by side, each tracking a different time. I need this."

The seller nodded, eyes gleaming like embers. "That's a traveler's watch. Keeps you grounded in two places at once, so you never lose your way."

Sadie grinned. "I'll take it."

"And what about you, girl?" The seller's gaze bore into mine, ancient and knowing. "This pendant might just save your skin."

I swallowed and nodded. "I'll take it."

I handed her my credit card, noticing her short, ragged nails and calloused palm. Then she looked at me, with clear, compassionate eyes. "I'd offer to box this up for you," she said, "but I think you should wear it."

I slipped the chain over my head and turned to leave. An uneasy sensation prickled the back of my neck. I glanced back, intending to give the woman one last look.

But she was gone.

I blinked, eyes scanning the market for a hint of where she might have gone. In her place, I caught a fleeting glimpse of light—a soft, ethereal glow where the rustic booth had stood. Before I could fully process what I was seeing, the glow faded, leaving behind only the faint sound of a harp in the distance.

"Where did she go?" I whispered, turning to Sadie.

Sadie's brow furrowed as she scanned the area. "Who?"

"The woman who sold us these timepieces."

Sadie cocked her head at me, a half-smile forming on her lips. "You're kidding me, right? This necklace was a gift from my grandmother. I don't know where you got yours, but you've worn it for as long as I've known you. I always thought it was cool that you and I had similar necklaces."

Sadie always did have a strange sense of humor.

As we wove through the Wizards Market, the booths and tents around us hummed with a life of their own. I caught sight of a familiar face near the square's center, seated at a table draped in deep purple velvet. It was Madame Endora, the enigmatic owner of *Enchantments*. She had been the one to predict my return to Enchanted Springs during my Saturn Return, so it wasn't surprising to find her here tonight, offering readings under the magic-soaked sky. But something about her seemed off.

Her usually sharp eyes were clouded, staring blankly at the flickering candle before her. Her movements were slow, deliberate, almost mechanical, as if she were a marionette controlled by invisible strings. The sight sent a cold prickle across my skin, raising the fine hairs on my arms.

"Look, there's Madame Endora," I whispered to Sadie, who was busy inspecting a nearby stall. But she didn't seem to hear me, her focus entirely absorbed in some shimmering trinket. I turned my gaze back to Madame Endora, taking a hesitant step toward her table.

As if sensing my presence, her head snapped up, eyes locking onto mine. For a heartbeat, the world around me faded, and it was just the two of us in the eerie glow of the market's lanterns. She reached out with a hand that shook ever so slightly, plucking a single card from the fan of tarot cards spread before her. Holding it up, she fixed me with an unnerving, glassy stare.

The Death card.

I froze, my breath catching in my throat. It wasn't the card itself that rattled me—Death usually signified transformation in tarot readings. But the image on this particular card sent icy tendrils creeping up my spine. The figure on the card was cloaked in black, skeletal hands gripping a scythe, with glowing red eyes peering out from the shadows of its hood.

The very same figure I had glimpsed at the edge of the market.

Madame Endora's lips curled into a slow, cryptic smile. When she spoke, her voice wasn't her own. It was dark, raspy, almost masculine—like gravel scraping against stone. "Not all endings are final, child," it croaked, the sound reverberating through the air like an ancient incantation. "But some reveal truths buried in the shadows."

The words echoed in my ears, a haunting riddle that tightened the knot of dread in my stomach. My breath hitched, and I glanced around wildly. Sadie was ambling ahead, her eyes gleaming with excitement for the movie, completely oblivious to the strangeness unfolding behind me.

I turned back to Madame Endora, but she was already changing. Her eyes blinked, the eerie haze lifting, and her posture relaxed as if waking from a deep, dark sleep. She stared at the card in her hand, confusion wrinkling her brow.

"What in the name of Hecate?" she muttered, her voice now her own—a rich, melodic tone that had guided many through the twists of fate. Her gaze shifted back to me, her eyes wide and questioning. "Who's been messing with my deck? Why is this card out?"

The question hung in the air like smoke. My throat tightened, words refusing to form as a chill swept over me, settling deep into my bones. Madame Endora's fingers fumbled to shuffle the Death card back into the deck, her movements hasty, almost frantic. I wanted to ask, to demand what had just happened, but the words stuck, a lump of fear lodged in my throat.

Just then, Sadie's voice rang out, cutting through the oppressive tension. "Come on, Marley! It's showtime!"

I turned toward her, my heart pounding against my ribs, willing my legs to move. "Coming!" I called, though my voice sounded distant, like it was coming from someone else entirely.

When I glanced back one last time, Madame Endora was staring into the candle's flame, a troubled look on her face. The market continued to bustle around us, but the darkness of that moment lingered, a shadow that refused to be shaken off.

CHAPTER 6

The Parthenon Theater

T HE PARTHENON THEATER STOOD like a crown jewel at
the end of Enchanted Avenue, its grand marquee glowing
in classic gold and white bulbs. The title of tonight's film, *Daggers and Disguises,* blazed across the marquee, casting an amber
glow over the throngs of people gathering outside.

The Parthenon had transformed into a Halloween spectable,
its stately brick exterior now draped in an array of spooky decorations. Cobwebs stretched from the theater's decorative cornices
to the arched windows, interlaced with glittering, giant plastic
spiders. The marquee itself was adorned with garlands of black
and purple tinsel.

On either side of the grand marquee, larger-than-life
jack-o'-lanterns grinned wickedly at passersby, their carved faces
illuminated from within by a ghostly, pulsing light. The theater's
main windows featured stained-glass decals depicting witches,
bats, and haunted houses in shades of blood red and deep purple.
Ghostly figures were painted onto the glass, giving the illusion

that specters lurked just behind the panes, watching the street below.

Lining the sidewalk, a row of tombstones had been set up, each inscribed with humorously macabre epitaphs like, "Here Lies a Dull Actor" and "Intermission – Back Soon." A few animatronic ghosts, placed strategically between the tombstones, periodically popped up with eerie wails, startling unsuspecting onlookers.

"Wow," Sadie murmured beside me, her eyes fixed on the decorations. "They've really outdone themselves this year."

Bouquets of deep purple calla lilies, blood-red roses, and spiky black dahlias filled antique urns that flanked the entrance, each bouquet a masterpiece of eerie elegance. Silver-dusted eucalyptus and curly willow branches twisted through the arrangements, giving them a wild, almost sinister beauty. The air was thick with the scent of sage, rosemary, and nightshade, the herbs tucked among the blooms adding an earthy, mystical fragrance.

We paused in front of the movie poster for *Daggers and Disguises*, a showstopper hanging just outside the theater. Rendered in black and white, it evoked the golden age of noir cinema with its vintage design. In the center, a shadowy figure stood shrouded in a long trench coat, the brim of a fedora casting a menacing shadow over a pair of piercing eyes. The figure held a gleaming dagger in one gloved hand, the blade reflecting a faint, almost spectral glow.

"Classic," Sadie breathed, leaning in for a closer look. "It's got that *Casablanca* vibe, but with a sinister edge."

My gaze traveled over the poster, taking in the faces of the film's characters, frozen in various expressions of fear, suspicion, and cunning. Smoke curled up from the poster's base, revealing the title in an elegant, calligraphic font: *Daggers and Disguises.* The tagline beneath it read, "In a world of secrets, every dagger has a story."

I shivered slightly, a thrill of anticipation running through me. "Perfect for tonight, don't you think?"

Sadie nodded, a small, eager smile playing on her lips. "Oh, absolutely. This movie is going to be a real treat."

We made our way up the theater steps, the scent of herbs and flowers intensifying with each step. The bouquets looked even more stunning up close; the roses glistened as if kissed by dew, and the dark, velvety dahlias gave off an almost otherworldly allure. I couldn't help but wonder if Joanna had cast a little magic of her own into them. With her, you could never quite tell where the line between art and enchantment blurred.

As we reached the top of the stairs, I paused to glance back at the crowd below. Costumed townsfolk and paranormal creatures mingled effortlessly, laughter and whispers rising on the cool October air. For tonight, at least, the worlds of the magical and the mundane danced hand in hand under the glow of the theater lights.

"Well, here we go," I said, turning back to Sadie as we stepped towards the entrance. "Time to see if the movie lives up to the hype."

She grinned, linking her arm through mine. "Or if there's more than meets the eye."

At the door, an attendant scanned our tickets. He wore a velvet cape and a top hat, tipping it graciously as he tore the stubs and waved us inside.

"Enjoy the show, ladies," he said, his eyes glinting mischievously. "It's bound to be unforgettable."

Sadie raised an eyebrow at me as we stepped into the lobby. "Well, that's not ominous at all."

Inside, the lobby unfolded before us like a scene from a Gothic fairy tale. Midnight-blue hydrangeas spilled over the edges of tall, gothic vases positioned on intricately carved tables, their blooms interwoven with strands of ivy and trailing black lace ribbons. Orange marigolds glowed like embers against clusters of white baby's breath, while tendrils of dried vines curled around them like skeletal fingers. The arrangements looked almost alive, as if they might reach out and wrap around an unsuspecting guest at any moment.

"They really went all out," I murmured, my eyes tracing the delicate artistry in the centerpieces. "It's like we're stepping into the movie itself."

Sadie nodded, her gaze sweeping the room. "She has a knack for the dramatic. I half expect a detective in a trench coat to walk in at any moment."

Gold-framed mirrors lined the walls, reflecting whimsical Halloween scenes that seemed to move within the glass—skeletons danced with phantoms, jack-o'-lanterns grinned mischievously, their eyes flickering with hidden secrets. Everything in the lobby was awash in shadows and silver hues, echoing the classic black-and-white films of the past.

Swathes of cobweb-like lace draped across the marble counters, and clusters of antique lanterns glowed in every corner, casting an eerie, otherworldly light. A grand staircase wrapped in rich black velvet dominated the room, each step adorned with faux candles flickering in shades of violet and gold, casting ghostly shapes on the walls.

"Look at those mirrors," Sadie whispered, clutching my arm. "It's like they're showing scenes from some long-lost film."

I glanced at the nearest mirror, half-expecting to see my own reflection. Instead, a pair of skeletons twirled through a waltz, their bony fingers entwined as they danced in front of a moonlit graveyard. A shiver ran down my spine. "This place is pure magic," I replied softly, feeling the hair on my arms stand on end.

The lobby bustled with costumed guests. Some clutched elaborately decorated masks, while others sported full get-ups that would've been right at home in a 1940s crime drama—sleek fedoras, double-breasted suits, evening gowns with fur stoles. The air hummed with laughter, clinking glasses, and snippets of excited conversation. The scent of buttered caramel popcorn mingled with the faint aroma of incense, adding to the theater's mystique.

"Can you believe this atmosphere?" Sadie whispered, eyes shining with excitement. "It's like we've stepped into the movie."

Before I could reply, a familiar figure floated gracefully through the crowd. Violet, in her smoky eye makeup and powdered face, glided past in her drop-waist dress, her beads swaying with every ethereal step. She paused to examine a towering candelabrum, her lips curving into a satisfied smile.

"She's a showstopper," I murmured. Most people around us glanced at Violet with admiration, assuming she was just another clever partygoer in a spectacular costume. Only Sadie and I knew the truth.

"Violet certainly knows how to make an entrance," Sadie quipped, a smirk tugging at the corner of her lips. "Think she'd get mad if I borrowed her look next year?"

I chuckled, unable to tear my eyes away from the scene unfolding around us. The flickering candlelight, the elegance of the decorations, the low hum of conversations—it was all too perfect. This wasn't just a theater lobby; it was a gateway to another era, a place where magic and mystery met in a dance as timeless as the movies themselves.

CHAPTER 7

Concessions & Confessions

THE LOBBY OF THE Parthenon was alive with the low hum of conversation and the soft clink of glasses. Near the ticket window, a quaint alcove served as the theater's concession stand for the evening. Framed by half walls on three sides, it was stocked with wine bottles arranged artfully on display. Behind it, a bartender in a crisp white shirt and vintage black vest poured glasses of wine and champagne with practiced ease.

Along the back wall, a small buffet table had been set up with Halloween-themed hors d'oeuvres. The spread was nothing short of gourmet: miniature pumpkin tarts dusted with cinnamon, deviled eggs topped with eerie olive "eyeballs," and tiny canapés layered with cream cheese, smoked salmon, and a sprinkle of caviar. The table was edged with garlands of twinkling fairy lights that cast a soft glow over the artful display.

The scent of freshly popped corn mingled with the buttery sweetness of caramel, drifting through the air like an irresistible lure. I turned, spotting the source: an old-fashioned popcorn cart parked in the corner. A striped awning in vibrant red and white,

41

gave it an air of vintage charm, along with brass accents that glinted under the chandelier's light. A hand-painted sign perched on top read, "Homemade Caramel Popcorn: A Halloween Treat!"

Sadie's eyes lit up the moment she caught sight of it. "Caramel popcorn? I can't resist." She made a beeline for the cart.

A theater volunteer, dressed as a classic movie usher in a scarlet jacket with gold buttons and a little black bow tie, stood next to the cart. His smile was warm as he scooped a fresh batch of popcorn into retro striped bags. The caramel-coated kernels glistened under the lobby lights, their rich, golden hue promising a decadent treat.

"Care for some popcorn?" he asked, offering one of the striped bags with a flourish.

Sadie nodded eagerly. "Yes, please! Two bags." She turned and nudged me playfully. "You're not getting out of this, Marley."

I laughed, unable to resist her enthusiasm. "All right, you win." I reached for one of the warm bags. The smell alone was intoxicating—a blend of butter, sugar, and toasted corn that transported me straight back to childhood Halloween nights.

Sadie wasted no time, popping a piece into her mouth with a sigh of pure delight. "Oh, this is heavenly," she declared, her eyes half-closed in pleasure. "It's got that perfect mix of crunchy and chewy."

I took a piece, savoring the way the caramel melted on my tongue, the subtle hint of sea salt balancing the sweetness. "You're right," I admitted, smiling as I glanced around the bustling lobby. "They really know how to do Halloween right."

Guests in elaborate costumes flowed around us, the lobby a blur of color and movement. I spotted a woman in an elegant ball gown, her face hidden behind a feathered mask, chatting animatedly with a man dressed as a detective in a fedora and trench coat. The whole scene felt like a glamorous masquerade, adding another layer of magic to the night.

We were halfway through our popcorn, laughing about how Violet was already the life of the party, when Sadie nudged me with her elbow.

"Hey, check it out," she whispered, her tone dripping with amusement. "Is that...?"

I turned to look in the direction she was pointing, expecting to see some over-the-top costume or one of the theater's themed decorations. What I saw instead made my jaw drop.

"Oh. My. God," I breathed, blinking hard as if to clear my vision. "No way!"

There they were—Grandma Clara and Eleanor, sweeping into the room like old Hollywood royalty. That in itself wasn't too shocking. They always had a flair for the dramatic, after all. But tonight, they weren't alone. Each of them was on the arm of a dashing escort, both men wearing tuxedos, looking as if they'd come straight from a Hollywood premiere.

Gram had gone full glamour, with a floor-length white gown that glimmered under the soft lighting. She looked like an ethereal goddess, her auburn hair piled high with a cluster of pearls glistening like stars. On her arm was a man who exuded charisma—a tall, silver fox with eyes that sparkled mischievously. Who was he? I squinted, noticing a faint shimmer around him, almost like he had a wizard's glow—an aura of magic that only those in our community could sense.

"Is this real life?" Sadie muttered, her eyes wide as saucers. "Your grandmother and Eleanor *both* brought dates?"

Eleanor had matched Gram's glamour with a red velvet gown. Her silver curls were styled to perfection, jeweled pins winking from the artful updo. And walking beside her? An equally distinguished gentleman, complete with a perfectly trimmed mustache and an air of suave mystery. He had that same magical shimmer, a subtle light that suggested more than just human charm.

I quickly ran through the past week's conversations in my head. Not once had they mentioned dates. In fact, they'd implied they were going to the movie "together," just the two of them. I shot a look at Sadie, who looked equally stunned.

"Nope, this was definitely not in the plans," I whispered back, eyes glued to the scene unfolding in front of us. "Where did they find these guys? Did they just conjure them or something?"

"Wouldn't put it past 'em," Sadie muttered, half in awe and half in disbelief.

As they approached, Clara caught my eye and waved with her free hand, a playful smile on her lips that seemed to say, *Caught you off guard, didn't I?*

"Well, Marley," she trilled, her voice rich with amusement, "don't just stand there with your mouth open! I'd like you to meet Humberto." She gestured to the charming man on her arm, who gave me a sly wink. The faint glow around him flickered like candlelight, hinting at some magical lineage.

I snapped my jaw shut, finding my voice. "Hi, Humberto," I managed, my mind still racing. "Nice to meet you."

"And this is Edward," Eleanor added, presenting her own dashing companion. Edward inclined his head, a glint of humor in his eyes that matched the subtle, mystical aura around him.

"Pleasure," he said smoothly. "Eleanor has spoken of you often."

"Oh, she has, has she?" I replied, shooting a glance at Eleanor, who merely arched an elegant eyebrow as if daring me to ask how she'd managed this little coup.

Beside me, Sadie let out a laugh. "Well, well. Looks like you two have been busy. Here I thought we were the ones making plans for tonight."

Clara's eyes twinkled. "One must always be prepared for surprises—especially on Halloween."

With that, they swept past us, their escorts leading them toward the bar. Sadie and I exchanged looks of disbelief.

"I can't believe it," I whispered, shaking my head. "They didn't tell us a thing."

"They're sneaky, I'll give them that," Sadie replied, grinning despite herself. "But hey, props to them. We just got outshone by the grandmas."

"Completely," I admitted, still stunned but undeniably impressed.

Sadie looped her arm through mine, a mischievous gleam in her eyes. "Well, we might not have dates, but we do have acces to wine."

I led her toward the bar. "Here's to romance, intrigue, and our inevitable headache tomorrow."

CHAPTER 8

Spirits and Secrets

T HE BAR WAS TUCKED into an alcove behind the ticket counter, framed by half walls on three sides and lined with wine bottles. We stepped into line. My eyes scanning the selection of wines as I waited. The labels boasted everything from crisp Chardonnays to deep Merlots. Beside me, a woman caught my eye.

She was dressed in a deep-purple velvet gown, and her silver hair, styled in perfect retro finger waves, framed her face elegantly. A delicate strand of pearls hung around her neck, glinting softly in the light. She held a glass delicately between two fingers, her posture poised and practiced, with just a hint of sophistication.

"If you're looking for a red," she said smoothly, noticing my perusal, "I highly recommend the Cabernet."

I glanced at the wine display, spotting the most elegant one. "The *Château d'Éclipse*?" I asked, nodding toward the bottle. Its label featured an intricate, embossed design of a moon partially obscured by shadow.

"Oh, no," she replied, her practiced smile never faltering. "That's a private selection one of our board members brought in for personal enjoyment." She gestured gracefully to a different label on the counter. "But the Sable Ridge Cabernet is excellent. It's from Red Vale Vineyards in California. My husband and I visited there a few years ago," she added, her eyes softening at the memory. "The vineyard is nestled in Napa Valley, and they age their Cabernet in oak barrels. It has just the right amount of smokiness and depth—perfect for an evening like this. Pairs wonderfully with savory bites like those," she finished, nodding toward the buffet table where a spread of hors d'oeuvres were arranged."

I followed her gaze, noting the mini pumpkin tarts and deviled eggs with olives. The little delicacies shimmered enticingly under the candlelight. "Sounds like a recommendation I can trust," I said, giving her a warm smile.

She nodded graciously before turning to join a distinguished gentleman who was standing with a small group. He looked every bit the gangster from a classic noir film—charcoal-gray pinstripe suit, fedora tipped at a rakish angle, and a crisp white shirt that contrasted sharply against his dark attire. His loose tie hung carelessly around his neck, lending him a devil-may-care appearance that invited both intrigue and skepticism.

In one hand, he casually toyed with a small prop switchblade, flicking it open and closed as he talked. The blade caught the light each time it snapped out, a glint of silver that added an edge to his otherwise relaxed demeanor. His other hand cradled a glass of red wine, which he swirled lazily, letting the liquid catch the dim light in rich, ruby tones. He seemed at ease, his grin sharp and playful as he laughed with those around him.

His gaze shifted to me, and for a moment, our eyes met. He reached up to tilt his fedora in a slow, deliberate movement, and winked at me.

Ew.

Luckily, I was up next.

The bartender stood behind the counter, sleeves rolled to his elbows, a dark vest snug over his crisp white shirt. He looked every bit the part of a vintage barkeep, right down to the bow tie and slicked-back hair. His thin mustache twitched slightly as he polished a glass, giving him the look of someone who had stepped out of a noir film.

"Evening, ladies," he greeted us with a nod. "What'll it be?"

"So, are you going to go for the Cabernet?" Sadie whispered, nudging me out of my brief reverie.

"Yeah," I said, turning back to the bartender. "Two glasses of the Sable Ridge Cabernet, please."

"Coming right up." His calm demeanor was a soothing contrast to the lively buzz of the lobby.

The bartender nodded and began to pour, his movements steady and practiced, the wine cascading into our glasses with a smooth, almost musical gurgle. He handed one to me and the other to Sadie with a practiced flourish.

"Enjoy the show," he said.

"To mysteries and moonlight," Sadie toasted, raising her glass.

"And to unexpected surprises," I added, glancing one last time at the couple.

CHAPTER 9

Enter the Vampire

J UST THEN, JACK EDGEWOOD made his entrance, gliding
into the lobby with a kind of effortless grace that only a vampire detective could pull off. He moved with quiet confidence, his gaze sweeping the room like a spotlight illuminating every corner.

Tonight, he had fully embraced his inner *Phantom of the Opera*—clad in a sharp vintage tuxedo with a red-lined cape draped over his broad shoulders and a half-mask that made his baby-blue eyes seem even more piercing.

He looked like something out of a time-travel romance novel, which, given his backstory, made perfect sense. Jack had been a beat cop in Chicago in the 1920s. He'd been turned into a vampire after a bootlegger shot him. The transformation had frozen him in that era. Detective Edgewood would forever be a dashing figure, with dark blond hair slicked back in a style that screamed old-world elegance. Tall, strong, and blessed with impossibly sharp features, he could have passed as a matinee idol—if not for his detective's no-nonsense demeanor.

I knew from experience that he could size up a room and catalog every suspicious glance, every fleeting gesture, in the blink of an eye. Jack wasn't just Enchanted Springs' resident vampire; he was its most intrepid investigator. Straight-laced, methodical, and about as dry as a chalkboard eraser, Jack had a way of cutting straight through nonsense with the efficiency of a razor-sharp knife. He didn't mince words. He didn't indulge in small talk. He was all business—usually, anyway.

"Evening, Miss Montgomery." His tone was serious, his cadence clipped. The corners of his mouth twitched, threatening to become a smile, but he kept it reined in.

I grinned, unable to resist teasing him. "Nice cape, Jack. Here to take a bite out of crime?" It was an old joke, something we both knew I trotted out on occasions like this. His expression remained impassive, but I caught the faintest glimmer of amusement in his eyes.

"Quite the event tonight," he replied, ignoring the jab but letting his eyes continue their methodical scan of the room. He missed nothing, his gaze landing briefly on the bartender, the woman in purple, and the movie poster at the far end of the lobby. I knew that look; Jack was already cataloging the scene, taking mental notes like a film noir detective.

"You have no idea," I muttered, casting my own glance around the room. "And here I thought this was just going to be a simple movie night."

Jack's mouth finally quirked into a half-smile, the kind that made him look more human—almost. "Things are rarely simple in Enchanted Springs."

We stood beside a particularly elaborate floral arrangement—a swirl of dark leaves and pale blossoms, all artfully arranged in shades of black, white, and purple. "Foxgloves," I said. "What a perfect choice for Halloween."

He turned his attention back to me, his eyes narrowing thoughtfully. "You picking up on anything unusual?"

I shrugged, not sure how much to say just yet. "The usual," I replied, keeping my tone light. "Spooky vibes, a Grim Reaper wandering at large, and enough paranormal energy to light up Main Street for a week. You?"

He nodded curtly, processing the information like data points in a spreadsheet. "Nothing out of the ordinary—yet. But it's early." He flicked a glance toward Sadie, who was busy examining her new bracelet, a faint glow emanating from its tiny stars. "You two sticking together tonight?"

"Like glue," I confirmed, catching his gaze again. "Just in case things get interesting."

His eyes softened, a flicker of concern passing through. "Good. Keep an eye out, both of you."

I nodded and took a sip of my Cabernet.

Conversation in the lobby was reaching a crescendo, mixing with the clink of wine glasses and the soft rustling of elegant costumes. Suddenly, a deep, resonant sound reverberated through the room, causing conversation to still for a split second. The echo lingered, almost like a spell casting silence over the crowd.

I turned toward the source, spotting a small brass gong mounted on an ebony stand near the entrance to the auditorium. Its surface gleamed under the soft glow of a nearby chandelier, intricate engravings catching the light with each ripple of sound. Beside the gong stood an usher in classic theater attire, his white-gloved hand still clutching the mallet. He gave a courteous bow, signaling the end of the lobby's mingling and the beginning of the night's cinematic adventure.

"That's our signal," I said to Sadie, nodding toward the small crowd now shuffling eagerly toward the theater doors. "Time to grab our seats." The air around us buzzed with anticipation, the final gong still echoing faintly as we joined the procession. En masse, we drifted toward the double doors that led to the main auditorium. I could already hear the faint strains of classical music drifting from within, heightening the sense of anticipation.

Just as we approached the doors, I spotted a dark figure near the grand staircase at the far end of the lobby. I froze, my gaze locking onto a shadow gliding halfway up the stairs to the balcony. The figure was unmistakable—the Grim Reaper again, the same cloaked form I'd glimpsed earlier at the Wizards Market. His cloak flowed around him like a living shadow, its edges curling in the dim light as if resisting definition. Beneath the hood, his face was obscured, swallowed by darkness.

A chill crept down my spine. He moved with an unnatural grace, gliding rather than walking, slipping into the darkness at the top of the stairs. I felt a jolt of alarm and grabbed Sadie's arm, my grip tight. "Sadie, do you see that?" I hissed, nodding toward the staircase.

She squinted, her expression shifting from curiosity to mild irritation. "See what? It's too dark over there."

"The Reaper," I whispered urgently, unable to tear my eyes away from the staircase. "He's heading up to the balcony."

Sadie sighed, half-amused, half-skeptical. "Marley, it's Halloween. Everyone's in costume. It's probably just someone being theatrical. You know how people get when there's an audience."

"Maybe," I muttered, my stomach twisting with unease. But deep down, I knew this was different. He moved too smoothly. He wasn't just dressed for the part—he was the part. The shadows clung to him, and for a heartbeat, it felt as if he belonged to them in a way that defied the merriment around us.

Sadie gave my arm a reassuring pat. "Come on. Let's not let some creepy costume ruin our night. The movie's starting."

Reluctantly, I let her lead me through the double doors, casting one last glance back at the staircase. But the Grim Reaper had vanished, swallowed by the shadows of the balcony above.

CHAPTER 10

The Heart of the Theater

AS WE ENTERED THE Parthenon's grand auditorium, ushers in red jackets and gold buttons handed everyone a folded playbill. Each playbill was a miniature work of art, its cover depicting the dagger-wielding figure from the movie poster, surrounded by curling vines and shadowed alleyways.

I stepped into the theater and gasped. In every corner, Halloween decorations added an enchanting layer to the theater's historic elegance. Black candelabras with flickering faux candles lined the aisles, and clusters of ghostly white lilies sat on the edge of the stage. The Parthenon had transformed into a perfect blend of old-world glamour and supernatural allure.

Red velvet seats curved gracefully toward the stage, arranged in perfect symmetry. The hushed murmur of the crowd mingled with the stirring notes of classical music, drifting from hidden speakers to set the mood. The stirring strains of Danse Macabre began to swell through the auditorium, filling the air with an eerie, haunting beauty.

Sadie squeezed my arm as we followed the usher to our row, her eyes wide with excitement. "This is magnificent," she whispered, her gaze sweeping across the grand hall. "It's like stepping back in time."

And it was. For tonight, the Parthenon wasn't just a theater; it was a portal to another era, dressed in red velvet, gilded gold, and the haunting magic of Halloween.

Above us, the theater's crown jewel gleamed: a massive crystal chandelier, with thousands of facets, that sent tiny rainbows dancing across the ceiling. The chandelier hung proudly from the center, its gold-plated arms curved and graceful, draped in garlands of ivy and tiny fairy lights that twinkled like stars against the gleaming crystals. Tonight, thanks to a bit of theater magic, shadows resembling bats and spiders flickered and danced across the ceiling, giving the room an added air of mystery.

The ceiling itself was a masterpiece, painted in a faux fresco style to mimic the elegance of an Italian palace. Swirling clouds of soft pink and gold framed a vivid, mythical scene of ancient gods and muses looking down from an imagined heavenly scape. Gilded ornamentation lined the perimeter, adding a touch of grandeur to the room, while intricate plasterwork framed every arch and alcove.

The proscenium arch surrounding the stage was a display of artistry in itself, its gilded moldings now intertwined with ivy and twinkling lights. The heavy red velvet curtains hung elegantly in front, their lush folds framing the stage like a gateway to a bygone era.

Flanking the stage were two swanky private boxes, draped in cobweb lace and crowned with clusters of black roses. Their velvet curtains, tied back with golden cords, added a touch of regal charm to the scene. I nudged Sadie when I noticed who was sitting in the box to the right: Clara, Eleanor, and their dashing dates.

The music's crescendo matched my rising anticipation. It was as if the whole auditorium held its breath, waiting for the night's mysteries to unfold.

I scanned the room again. Jack Edgewood had just slipped into his seat a few rows ahead of us, his keen gaze scanning the crowd before locking eyes with me. He gave me a subtle nod, his expression unreadable. I knew that look. Jack's vampire senses were on high alert.

I shifted in my seat, a prickle of unease crawling up my neck. We were seated in the center of the theater, and I had a clear view of the whole auditorium. I scanned the rows of seats, a sea of shadowed faces illuminated by the ghostly glow of the screen. My gaze traveled up to the balcony, where I could just make out the darkened shape of the Grim Reaper figure from before. He was still there, standing motionless, his gaze seemingly locked onto the scene below. A cold shiver ran down my spine.

"Look at him," I whispered to Sadie, nodding toward the balcony. She squinted in the direction of my gaze but shook her head.

"Marley, it's just someone in costume. Get over it, already."

CHAPTER 11

The Playbill

S ADIE NUDGED ME, HER eyes gleaming as she pointed at the open playbill in her hands. "Check this out," she whispered. "It's a synopsis."

> *During a Halloween masquerade ball* in post-war Paris, a cursed dagger changes hands with each twist of the plot. The story follows an enigmatic femme fatale, an ex-convict seeking revenge, and a detective whose mask hides more than just his face. As costumed revelers—witches, phantoms, and monsters—whirl through candlelit ballrooms and fog-shrouded alleyways, sinister forces match their steps.

"Sounds juicy." Sadie's eyes sparkled with excitement. "A Halloween masquerade, secrets, and daggers? Perfect for tonight!"

"Definitely," I agreed, though a strange sense of foreboding settled over me. The film's atmosphere—dark, ominous, steeped in secrets—mirrored the unsettling energy of the night. My mind wandered back to the Grim Reaper I'd seen earlier, the shadowy figure gliding up the staircase like an omen. It was almost as if the movie and reality were beginning to blur, threads of fiction weaving into the fabric of our evening.

I flipped to the next page, which had illustrations of the movie's most iconic scenes. The dagger appeared in nearly every image, glinting dangerously in candlelit rooms or clutched in the shadows by gloved hands. One particularly striking image depicted the grand ballroom, masked dancers swirling beneath a massive chandelier, while at the center stood a figure in a Grim Reaper costume, holding the dagger aloft. Its blade gleamed in the dim, flickering light, casting eerie shadows across the page. I couldn't shake the feeling that the imagery in this movie was all too close to what I'd seen tonight.

I looked around, my mind still spinning with the images and synopsis. Secrets, lies, and daggers. The movie hadn't even started, and yet, the tension in the room felt like the opening chords of a suspenseful melody.

CHAPTER 12

A Cold-Blooded Welcome

T HE HOUSE LIGHTS DIMMED, the music stopped, and a hush fell over the audience. For a moment, the theater was bathed in darkness. Then, a single spotlight flared to life, casting a pool of light on the stage. In that glowing circle stood a woman, her silhouette striking against the shadowy backdrop.

She wore a strapless evening gown of sleek black velvet that clung to her figure, the fabric shimmering subtly under the spotlight. Long, satin gloves stretched past her elbows, adding an air of old Hollywood glamour. Her raven hair, styled in luxurious waves, cascaded past her shoulders, a side part creating a soft veil over one eye. Around her wrist, a delicate silver bracelet caught the light—a hint of sparkle against her otherwise dark, dramatic ensemble.

"Good evening, everyone!" she called, her voice echoing warmly through the theater. "I'm Joanna Elliott, director of the Parthenon Theater, and it's my privilege to welcome you to the annual Monsters on Main midnight matinee!"

63

She paused, a glint of humor in her eyes. "Now, as you all know, we've scheduled this event to wrap up by midnight, because—let's face it—it's a school night. And, unfortunately, we all have to return to our regular lives tomorrow." A ripple of laughter moved through the audience, a shared, knowing chuckle that eased the tension in the room.

Her voice was smooth, almost hypnotic, drawing every eye to her. "Tonight's screening is special indeed. Seventy-five years after its premiere, the classic murder mystery *Daggers and Disguises* returns to the Parthenon."

She paused, allowing her words to settle over the crowd like the velvet curtain behind her.

Her ruby-painted lips curved into a knowing smile as she continued, her voice dropping to a sultry purr. "Ah, yes. Tonight, we are embracing the thrill of secrets, the allure of hidden identities, and the danger that lurks in the shadows." Her eyes swept over the audience, catching the glint of light as she moved. "This film is a masterpiece of intrigue, where nothing—and no one—is quite what they seem. How fitting, wouldn't you agree, for an evening like Halloween?"

The audience chuckled softly, some nodding in agreement. Joanna's eyes glittered under the spotlight as she leaned forward slightly, adding a conspiratorial tone to her voice. "Now, you might wonder, what lies behind the masks we all wear tonight? Which of us carries a dagger hidden in our sleeve?" She laughed lightly, but the question lingered in the air, sending a shiver through the room.

"But enough teasing," she said, straightening, her posture impeccable. "Tonight is all about the magic of the movies, the art of illusion, and yes, a little danger." Her gaze turned toward the projectionist's booth, and with a sweeping gesture of her gloved arm, she declared, "So, let's start the screening, shall we? The night is young, and our tale of *Daggers and Disguises* awaits. Sit back, enjoy, and remember—on Halloween, the line between reality and fantasy is thinner than you think."

With a final, enigmatic smile, she turned and glided offstage, the click of her heels punctuating the stillness left in her wake. The spotlight faded, and darkness enveloped the theater once more, filling the room with a collective breath of anticipation.

CHAPTER 13

Darkness Falls

T HE LIGHTS DIMMED, PLUNGING the room into darkness. The hum of anticipation was almost palpable as the projection screen was lowered on stage. A hush fell over the audience, followed by the faint click of the projector spinning to life.

Light sliced through the room, casting flickering shadows that crawled up the theater walls. A haunting orchestral score filled the air, its low, ominous notes setting the stage for *Daggers and Disguises.*

On screen, the opening credits rolled in elegant, old-fashioned script, drenched in shadows and mystery. As the scene shifted to a foggy street corner in post-war Paris, the air around me thickened.

I glanced around, catching glimpses of faces bathed in the eerie glow of the silver screen. Clara and Eleanor, seated in their private box, leaned forward, completely engrossed. Between them sat an extravagant charcuterie board draped with slices of prosciutto, creamy brie, and clusters of grapes. Clara casually reached for an olive, popping it into her mouth with an air of refined nonchalance, while Eleanor speared a wedge of smoked gouda, her eyes still fixed on the screen.

Sadie, beside me, was already captivated, her eyes wide as she followed every flicker of movement on screen. The room had fallen into a collective trance, everyone drawn into the movie's spell.

The flickering images painted the theater in shades of black, white, and grey. Shadows danced along the ornate ceiling, mingling with the faux-painted cherubs and ivy that twined around the chandelier's golden chain. The air grew cooler, and the scent of aged upholstery mixed with the scent of wine to create a heady concoction that only added to the atmosphere. It was as if the Parthenon itself had become an extension of the movie, a living, breathing noir film.

I tried to settle into my seat, but an uneasy tension knotted in my stomach. The room felt alive—more so than usual. Around me, people whispered in hushed tones, their eyes flicking back and forth between the screen and their companions. I caught sight of a few costume masks glinting in the dim light, their hollow eyes staring back at the screen with an intensity that sent chills down my spine.

The movie unfolded like a masterwork of suspense. A femme fatale appeared on screen, her eyes smoldering as she crept through shadowed alleys, her movements smooth and feline. The audience leaned in, some clutching the armrests of their seats. I could feel the tension ratcheting up with every scene, every flicker of candlelight on the screen.

I glanced a few rows ahead, where Joanna had taken a seat beside the man in the fedora. He held a glass of wine in one hand. The light from the screen cast his face in an unsettling pallor, while Joanna's eyes glinted sharply in the darkness, fixed on the movie. Their body language suggested a certain familiarity, but the way she occasionally darted glances at him suggested something more complicated. My skin prickled with unease as I turned back to the screen.

The film's grainy, black-and-white imagery painted a world of shadows and secrets. A dagger glinted ominously on screen, and the audience gasped in unison. Was it just my imagination, or was the man next to Joanna flicking his switchblade too?

He was. I could see light glinting from its blade.

In the film, the camera panned to a grand ballroom filled with masked revelers, all cloaked in secrets. The protagonist moved through the dancers, dagger gleaming in his hand, every step echoing with the soundtrack's ominous crescendos. Around me, I felt the audience collectively hold their breath. It was as if we were all part of the scene, infiltrating the ballroom alongside the characters on screen.

"Do you feel like something's off?" I whispered to Sadie, keeping my voice low.

Sadie barely tore her eyes from the screen, her brow furrowing ever so slightly. "It's a Halloween movie, Marley," she murmured. "Everything's supposed to feel off. It's part of the allure."

I scanned the room again. Every face around me was alight with the glow of the screen, eyes wide and mouths slightly agape, mirroring the film's mounting tension. I caught a glimpse of Violet, who had joined Clara and Eleanor in their box. In the flickering light, her pancake makeup and smoky eyeshadow made her face look like a skull.

CHAPTER 14

Dark Shadows

B EHIND US, IN THE balcony, shadows pooled in the corners. My gaze flicked upward, expecting to see nothing, but instead, I caught a glimpse of something moving—a dark shape slipping further into the shadows. The Grim Reaper? I blinked, straining to see more, but the darkness swallowed him whole. My heart thudded in my chest, and I forced my eyes back to the screen.

The scene shifted, now showing the villain in a dimly lit room. He raised a gleaming dagger high, its blade reflecting the candlelight. A murmur swept through the audience, a mix of gasps and nervous laughter. In that instant, I glanced around again, noticing couples gripping each other's hands, their knuckles white, as they sat frozen in their seats. The room crackled with a tension that went beyond the movie.

"Do you feel it?" I whispered to Sadie, trying to keep my voice steady. "Something's off."

"It's a noir film, Marley. Of course it's off," Sadie replied, still fixated on the screen. "That's the point."

"Right," I muttered, though the nagging sense of dread gnawed at me. My eyes drifted toward Joanna's companion. He lounged casually, the switchblade still in hand, occasionally lifting his glass of wine to his lips. Beside him, Joanna's eyes flickered between the movie and the knife, her fingers tapping restlessly on her armrest.

Couples huddled closer, their eyes reflecting the flickering light of the silver screen. I noticed some familiar faces—humans and paranormals alike—intermixed in the audience.

Toward the back, a woman sat perfectly still, her long, silver hair cascading over her shoulders. She turned her head slightly, and I caught a glimpse of her eyes—glowing faintly like the moon itself. A fae, unmistakable, even though she had chosen to appear almost human tonight.

Nearby, a man in a crisp black suit whispered something to his companion. When he smiled, his lips curled back to reveal a flash of fangs, catching the screen's dim glow. I recognized him as one of the local vampires who frequented my shop for antique mirrors.

Closer to the aisle, a figure in a green velvet cloak adjusted his collar, revealing a faint scale pattern that glinted briefly before disappearing beneath his clothes. A dragonkin, no doubt. I'd seen his kind in the market earlier, their eyes a shade too bright, their movements too fluid to belong to ordinary people. Here, on Halloween night, even the most elusive creatures came out to blend with the humans, masks discarded.

And there, just two rows ahead of me, a young woman with dark curls shifted in her seat, her movements graceful, almost feline. Her eyes glowed amber for the briefest of moments as the movie screen flickered. A shapeshifter, I noted silently.

The movie's tension gripped the room like a vise, tightening with every scene. Faces around me were lit in stark relief by the flickering screen—eyes wide, mouths slightly agape. People clutched their armrests, some nervously tapping their fingers, others clutching their drinks like talismans. Couples exchanged glances filled with a mixture of delight and trepidation, as if they were daring each other to embrace the thrill of the unknown.

On screen, the femme fatale pressed a gloved hand against the hero's chest, her eyes gleaming with secrets. The music swelled, dark and ominous, as the villain crept into view, brandishing a dagger that caught the light in a dazzling arc. A collective intake of breath swept through the audience.

The movie's soundtrack swelled, a haunting melody that sent chills rippling down my spine. The villain on screen advanced toward the masked protagonist, dagger gleaming ominously. In the darkness around me, I heard the rustle of clothing, the sound of someone shifting nervously in their seat, the soft clink of glasses. I took a deep breath, trying to focus on the film, but my senses remained on high alert.

As the film's tension built to a crescendo, I felt the energy in the room shift. The air grew electric, charged with fear and excitement. The scene on screen grew darker, the music climbing toward an eerie crescendo. My heart pounded in sync with the movie's rhythm.

Then, just as the villain raised the dagger high, the screen went black.

CHAPTER 15

Intermission

THE SUDDEN DARKNESS WAS shocking, and a collective gasp cut through the charged atmosphere like a blade. The tension in the room was palpable, hanging like a thick fog over the plush velvet seats.

I blinked, disoriented, as the house lights suddenly flooded the auditorium, casting a harsh glare over the audience. For a heartbeat, no one moved.

The abrupt brightness snapped us out of the movie's spell. Audience members blinked, disoriented, as they turned to each other.

"That was intense," Sadie exhaled, running a hand through her hair. "I could feel it in my bones."

I nodded, glancing toward the rows of guests now stretching and starting to stand. "Yeah, it was. Do you want another glass of ..."

My voice trailed off as I noticed Joanna, standing in the aisle, her face ashen.

"Larry!" she screamed, her voice slicing through the room like a knife. "Larry! What's wrong?"

A ripple of shock surged through the theater. Everyone turned to the slumped form in his seat. Larry's head lolled to one side, his eyes wide and unblinking. Time seemed to freeze for an agonizing second, the world holding its breath as the reality of the situation sank in.

This wasn't part of the show.

CHAPTER 16

A Sudden Ending

"**L**ARRY! LARRY, WAKE UP!"

Joanna had her hand on his shoulder, shaking him gently. Larry's head was hanging at an awkward angle, lolling slightly as she shook him.

Time stretched, moving as if through molasses. My breath hitched, and I was on my feet before I even realized it. From where I stood, I could only see the side of his face, pale and motionless. I searched for his switchblade. Had he been stabbed?

A murmur swelled around us, a wave of confusion and fear spreading through the crowd. Every sound seemed amplified: the rustle of fabric as he knelt, the creak of the seats as onlookers strained to get a better look.

In the next instant, Jack Edgewood was at his side. I didn't even see him approach; during a crisis, he moved at preternatural speed.

The moment stretched on, each second loaded with uncertainty. I pushed my way down the aisle, moving almost instinctively to Jack's side. We had worked two murder cases together before, and I knew that in this moment, his vampire senses were giving him an insight none of us could grasp.

My stomach turned as I finally saw Larry's face. His lips were a ghastly shade of blue, and his skin had taken on a waxy, pallid hue. His eyes were half-closed, glassy, staring blankly at nothing. A dark stain marred his lap where the wine glass had spilled.

Jack inhaled sharply, his nostrils flaring. His vampire senses were at work.

"We need a doctor!" Joanna's voice rose above the murmur of the crowd, her tone rising to near hysteria. "Is there a doctor in the house?"

For a moment, no one moved. Then, almost in a daze, a man stepped forward from the middle of the crowd, yanking off the plastic horns of his devil costume as he hurried down the aisle. "I'm a doctor," he announced, his voice cracking the tension like a whip. He knelt beside Larry, his fingers moving to the side of the man's neck. I held my breath, my heart hammering in my chest.

The doctor's eyes flicked up to Jack's, grim and steady. "I'm sorry," he said quietly, shaking his head. "He's gone."

A ripple of shock and horror moved through the room, a collective gasp from the audience. I glanced around, catching flashes of faces bathed in the harsh overhead light: some wide-eyed, others pressing hands to their mouths. This was no movie. This was reality, stark and unavoidable.

Jack's eyes narrowed, focusing on the wine glass lying on Larry's thigh. It still held a small amount wine, the deep red liquid shimmering under the dim lights of the theater.

Jack moved with deliberate calm, pulling a handkerchief from his coat pocket and wrapping it around the glass's stem before carefully lifting it. For a second, I glimpsed his eyes—sharp, calculating, as if piecing together a puzzle that only he could see.

"Ladies and gentlemen," Jack's voice rang out, smooth and controlled, cutting through the chaos in the room. "The show is over."

Silence fell, heavy and oppressive, broken only by the rustling of clothes as people shifted in their seats.

Joanna staggered back a step, her face a mask of confusion. "What happened? How—"

Jack raised a hand, signaling for quiet. "I need everyone to remain calm," he continued, his tone laced with a steel that brooked no argument. "What we have here appears to be a death under suspicious circumstances."

My gaze darted to the wine glass in Jack's hand. Poison. It had to be. I turned my eyes back to Jack, catching his subtle nod.

He leaned closer to me, his voice low. "Digitalis," he murmured, his eyes never leaving the dead man's face. "I'd bet on it. I caught a whiff the moment I got close."

CHAPTER 17

It's Curtains

I STEPPED BACK IN shock. Not a stabbing. Not some dramatic crime of passion. A calculated poisoning.

Jack's jaw tightened as he glanced around the theater, his gaze lingering on the shadows in the corners. I expected him to pull out his phone, call for backup, and lock this place down, but he didn't make a move.

"Shouldn't we call someone?" I asked hesitantly.

He shook his head, eyes sharp, nostrils flaring. "Not this time," he muttered, his voice low. "This isn't a normal crime scene, Marley."

Jack squared his shoulders, his eyes scanning the theater, piecing together the details. Then, he turned to me, his expression sharp, voice low. "This is Larry Linwood, president of the Parthenon's board of directors. I don't know the whole story yet, but I guarantee you there's more going on here than meets the eye. If this was a targeted poisoning, we need to contain the scene and focus on those with direct access to the glass. For now, we need to clear out everyone but the staff."

My mind spun, trying to connect the dots. Who had the opportunity? Who had the motive? Almost everyone in the lobby had access to the wine—but the theater staff had been closest.

I nodded, understanding his strategy. "Right," I agreed, glancing toward the crowd, which was now buzzing with confusion. "The staff were in the lobby all evening. They're our best lead."

At that moment, Grandma Clara and Eleanor approached, their expressions a mix of concern and resolve. Their wizard escorts hung back a bit, eyes sharp and assessing the situation.

"How can we help?" Eleanor asked. Her voice was calm and steady.

Jack turned to them, giving a curt nod of acknowledgment. "Clara, Eleanor," he began, his tone firm, "I need you to manage the exit. Take everyone's names and contact information as they leave. Make sure they do so in an orderly fashion."

They nodded, and Grandma Clara's eyes flicked to mine in silent reassurance.

Jack then straightened, raising his voice to command the room's attention. "Ladies and gentlemen," he called out, his voice carrying over the murmur of the crowd. "I'm afraid our evening has taken an unexpected turn. I need everyone who isn't a member of the theater staff to please exit the auditorium."

The audience stilled, uncertainty rippling through them like a wave. Some glanced around in confusion, while others hesitated, clutching their coats and bags.

Jack addressed the crowd once more. "Leave your name and contact information at the door. Go home, and if we need to reach out, you'll hear from us tomorrow."

Slowly, the patrons began to shuffle out, murmuring among themselves. Clara and Eleanor, flanked by their wizard escorts, stood in the lobby with notepads in hand, efficiently recording names and contact information as everyone filed past.

I watched the crowd go, my nerves taut as a wire. This wasn't just a Halloween scare. This was murder, and I suddenly had a front-row seat.

CHAPTER 18

Exit, Stage Left

THE AIR IN THE theater hung thick with tension. The house lights had been turned up, casting an unforgiving brightness over the auditorium and the scattered audience members still lingering in their seats. Jack stood at the center of it all, his eyes sweeping the room. Beside him, I noticed a handful of theater staff hovering near the aisles, their faces a mix of confusion and concern.

A young man in a black polo shirt edged closer to Jack. His hands fidgeted with the edge of his sleeve, eyes darting nervously toward Larry's still form in the chair. "Do you need me to stay?" His voice was barely above a whisper.

Jack glanced over, his expression unreadable. "What's your name?"

"Tyler, sir," the projectionist replied, swallowing hard. "I just run the equipment."

Jack nodded, then turned to the others. A pair of ushers stood by the exit, clutching their flashlights, looking pale under the harsh lights. Near them, the ticket manager, a middle-aged woman with glasses perched on the tip of her nose, fiddled with the lanyard around her neck. Two more staff members—the ticket scanners—hovered, looking lost and confused.

"I want everyone to stay calm," Jack said, his voice even. "You're not in trouble, but I need to know where you were when this happened." He gestured toward Larry's body without looking at it.

The ticket manager stepped forward, clearing her throat. "We were all at our posts," she said, pushing her glasses up her nose. "The ushers were in the aisles, Tyler was in the projection booth, and I was in the lobby with the scanners."

Jack nodded slowly, his gaze traveling over each of their faces. They all looked genuinely shaken, their nerves frayed. "And you," he said, addressing the projectionist. "You were up in the booth the entire time?"

Tyler nodded. "Yes, sir. Didn't leave my spot. I swear."

"And the rest of you?" Jack asked, his eyes flicking to the ushers and the ticket staff.

The ushers exchanged glances, then nodded. "We were helping people find their seats. I don't think we noticed anything unusual."

"Right," Jack said, his voice firm but not unkind. "I believe you. You can all go home."

Relief washed over their faces, and they nodded quickly. The ticket manager ushered them out, herding them like a flock of sheep, their footsteps shuffling across the carpet.

As they disappeared through the exit, the atmosphere in the room seemed to grow heavier, more foreboding.

Jack turned to the remaining staff, his gaze firm. "Joanna, Frances, Robert—stay where you are. We need to speak with you."

CHAPTER 19

Background Briefing

JACK MOTIONED FOR ME to step aside, and we moved down the aisle. "Before we start questioning," he began, his voice low, "you should know who we're dealing with here. I've crossed paths with each of them during my time serving on the Enchanted Springs Cultural Council. Trust me, there's a story here."

I glanced over at the suspects. Joanna stood near the aisle, her posture stiff, arms wrapped around her midsection as if to hold herself together. Her eyes darted from one corner of the theater to the next, her lips pressed into a thin line.

"Joanna Elliott," Jack continued, his gaze fixed on her. "Director of the Parthenon. She's been the driving force behind every theater event for the past decade. A perfectionist with a reputation for control. Joanna and the victim? Well, let's just say they had a complicated relationship."

"She seems jumpy," I observed. "You think it's just nerves, or something else?"

Jack's expression remained unreadable. "That's what we need to find out."

Next to Joanna, the woman in purple stood with a stoic air, one hand clutching her purse, the other held loosely by her side. I remembered her from the bar in the lobby: her silver hair was styled in old-school finger waves, and the pearls around her neck gleamed faintly under the theater lights. She looked calm, but I noticed the way her gaze was fixed on the floor, avoiding eye contact with everyone around her.

"Frances Butner is the theater's treasurer," Jack explained. "She's meticulous with money—some say overly cautious. She's married, though her husband never accompanies her to these late-night events. She's probably nervous about the financial hit the theater will take after this disaster."

I nodded, studying Frances. Her face was a mask, betraying nothing—but the tension in her shoulders suggested more. She exuded an air of restraint, as if she were holding something back.

"And then there's Robert Haper," Jack said, nodding toward the bartender. "He's an attorney. Volunteers to run the bar at most events. Paid his way through law school working in nightclubs. Knows his way around a drink and around a courtroom."

"So, we've got a theater director with control issues, a treasurer who may be hiding something, and a bartender with a sharp legal mind," I summed up, glancing back at Jack. "Quite the ensemble cast."

Jack nodded, his eyes narrowing slightly. "Indeed. And now, it's time to see how well they can improvise under pressure."

Mind, Spirit, Science: A Journey of Personal Transformation

2024
Amari Rise Publishing
3315 San Felipe Rd #97 San Jose Ca 95135
www.amaririse.com

For information address: Amari Rise Publishing. 3315 San Felipe Rd #97, San Jose, CA 95135
Marilyn Randolph
Printed in the United States of America ISBN:
(eBook)
Publisher – Amari Rise Publishing.

Amari Rise Publishing
www.amaririse.com
Copyright © 2019 Marilyn Randolph
All rights reserved.

Table of Contents

Foreword: An Invitation to Transformation

In a world filled with constant change, uncertainty, and moments of pain, we seek something unchanging to anchor our lives. *Mind Spirit Science: A Journey of Personal Transformation* is a guide for those longing for growth grounded in biblical truth. Through scripture, reflection, and personal stories, this book offers more than advice—it provides a pathway to real, lasting transformation rooted in faith.

This journey is about embracing the power of God's promises, trusting Him in every season, and allowing His word to renew our hearts and minds. As you walk through each chapter, may you discover the strength and resilience that come from leaning into God's love, and may His promises sustain you, guiding you to live with purpose, hope, and unwavering faith.

Introduction: A Journey that Began with Faith

This book is born from my life's journey—a journey shaped by faith, resilience, and countless lessons in trusting God. Growing up, I never imagined the paths I would take, the mountains I would climb, or the valleys I would pass through. Yet, through it all, God was with me, guiding me even when I couldn't see the way forward.

Life has brought me both blessings and battles. From raising six wonderful children to facing the end of a marriage I thought would last forever, I have learned that God's love and strength never fail. Moving from California to Atlanta and now to Florida, I found myself in a new season of life—one of quiet reflection and a deeper relationship with God.

In this season, I have discovered that true transformation comes from the inside out. It's not about changing our circumstances but allowing God to change us through His word. Just as He promises in **Romans 12:2**, we are transformed by the renewing of our minds. This book is my journey and my heart—a sharing of the scriptures, practices, and reflections that helped me walk through life's challenges with grace and faith.

In *Mind Spirit Science*, you'll find a path to personal growth, filled with practical tools and spiritual truths to help you on your journey. My hope is that, as you read, you'll find comfort in knowing that God walks with you too, ready to transform your heart and guide you in every season. So take a deep breath, trust in His love, and let the journey begin.

Opening Thoughts: Grounding in Faith

Transformation is at the heart of the Christian journey. In a world filled with challenges and uncertainties, we seek growth not through our own strength but through the renewing power of God. This book, *Mind Spirit Science: A Journey of Personal Transformation*, is a guide to experiencing deep, lasting change by anchoring ourselves in biblical truths and allowing God's wisdom to guide our steps.

Scriptural Foundation:

Romans 12:2 serves as the cornerstone of our journey:
"Do not conform to the pattern of this world, but be transformed by the renewing of your mind. Then you will be able to test and approve what God's will is—his good, pleasing, and perfect will."
Through this verse, we are reminded that true transformation happens when we surrender our thoughts and actions to God, allowing Him to reshape us into His image.

Life Experience:

Reflecting on my own journey, I've seen firsthand how God's word can guide us through life's most challenging moments. There was a time when I felt overwhelmed by the weight of my circumstances. Instead of finding answers in external solutions, I found strength in Romans 12:2, meditating on the power of renewing my mind. This simple but profound shift—looking to God for direction—became the foundation of my transformation. Through each step, I learned to lean on scripture as a source of strength and guidance.

Purpose of the Book:

This book is a tool for anyone who wants to walk in the purpose God has set for them. Each chapter will explore how biblical principles can help us build resilience, emotional wisdom, and a life filled with gratitude and purpose. It's about letting God's word shape us, trusting that He has a unique and powerful journey planned for each of us.

Chapter 1: Foundations of Transformation in Christ

Opening Reflection:

True transformation begins with a foundation rooted in Christ. Our journey to personal growth and resilience isn't about relying on our own strength but about leaning into God's promises. The Bible teaches us that, in Christ, we are new creations, constantly being renewed and strengthened. It's through this divine process that we can overcome challenges, build resilience, and live purposefully.

Scriptural Foundation:

A powerful scripture that defines our foundation in Christ is **2 Corinthians 5:17**:

"Therefore, if anyone is in Christ, he is a new creation. The old has passed away; behold, the new has come."

This verse reminds us that, as believers, we are made new in Christ. Transformation is not a one-time event but a continual journey, an ongoing renewal as we grow closer to God.

Building Resilience Through Faith:

When we face difficulties, the Bible encourages us to draw strength from God. In **Philippians 4:13**, we are reminded:

"I can do all things through Christ who strengthens me."

Whether we're facing a personal setback or a challenge in our relationships or careers, this verse serves as an anchor. Through Christ, we gain resilience—not because we are strong, but because He is.

Life Experience:
During a particularly challenging season of my life, I felt overwhelmed and unsure of where to turn. Through my prayer and study, **Philippians 4:13** kept surfacing, reminding me that I didn't have to carry my burdens alone. I began to trust that, with God's strength, I could overcome the obstacles before me. Each day, I repeated this verse, letting it become a source of courage and changes in your outlook or sense of peace. This practice builds a foundation of resilience, grounding you in God's word as you navigate life's challenges.

Conclusion of Chapter 1: resilience. This daily practice transformed my outlook and helped me see challenges as opportunities to grow in faith.

The Power of Faith-Filled Thinking:
God calls us to renew our minds, letting go of limiting beliefs and focusing on His promises. **Isaiah 26:3** speaks to this:
"You will keep in perfect peace those whose minds are steadfast, because they trust in you."
By centering our thoughts on God's faithfulness, we experience peace, resilience, and clarity. This peace is a foundation that

strengthens us from within, helping us to rise above the chaos and distractions of the world.

Practical Exercise:

Each day, take time to meditate on a scripture that speaks to your current struggles or needs. Reflect on verses like Philippians 4:13 or Isaiah 26:3, asking God to fill your mind with His truth. Write down your reflections and note any

Building our lives on Christ's foundation equips us to face life with confidence and strength. The world may shift and change, but God's word is steadfast. With this foundation, we can continue on our journey of transformation, knowing that we are never alone, and our strength is renewed daily through Him.

Chapter 2: The Mind and Spirit – Renewing Through Faith

Opening Reflection:

Transformation isn't only about external changes; it starts with renewing our mind and spirit. The Bible emphasizes the power of our thoughts and how our inner life shapes our actions, perspectives, and even our peace. As we choose to focus on God's truths and let go of negative or limiting beliefs, we create space for God's peace to enter our hearts.

Scriptural Foundation:

Romans 12:2 provides a powerful guide for mental and spiritual renewal:

"Do not conform to the pattern of this world, but be transformed by the renewing of your mind. Then you will be able to test and approve what God's will is—his good, pleasing and perfect will."

This verse reminds us that our thoughts and mindset have the power to transform us. By choosing to renew our mind with God's word, we align ourselves with His will and purpose.

Embracing Peace through Scripture:

God's word tells us that we can find true peace by focusing our thoughts on Him. **Isaiah 26:3** highlights this beautifully:

"You will keep in perfect peace those whose minds are steadfast, because they

trust in you."

When we center our thoughts on God's promises rather than on fear or worry, we experience a supernatural peace. This peace protects our hearts and minds, helping us navigate challenges with confidence.

Life Experience:

In my journey, there was a season when worry consumed my thoughts. I realized that my focus had drifted from God's promises to my own fears. Isaiah 26:3 became a source of strength for me. I made it a daily practice to meditate on this verse and remind myself to trust in God's goodness. Slowly, I felt His peace take root in my life, grounding me and easing my worries. This process of refocusing my mind helped me see challenges not as obstacles but as opportunities for faith.

Practical Steps for Renewing the Mind:

To renew our minds, we must actively choose thoughts that align with God's word. **Philippians 4:8** guides us on where to direct our focus:

"Finally, brothers and sisters, whatever is true, whatever is noble, whatever is right, whatever is pure, whatever is lovely, whatever is admirable—if anything is excellent or praiseworthy—think about such things."

This scripture reminds us to focus on thoughts that bring life and positivity, rather than those that drain or discourage us.

Exercise for Daily Renewal:

1. **Morning Meditation**: Start each day by reading a verse that speaks to you. Write it down and reflect on what it means to you personally.

2. **Redirecting Thoughts**: When a negative or anxious thought enters your mind, counter it with a scripture that provides truth and encouragement. Examples could include Philippians 4:13 ("I can do all things through Christ who strengthens me") or Psalm 23:1 ("The Lord is my shepherd; I shall not want").

3. **Evening Reflection**: End each day by reflecting on moments where you felt God's peace or guidance. Write down a verse that resonates and pray for continued renewal.

Conclusion of Chapter 2:

Renewing our mind is an ongoing journey that draws us closer to God, deepening our peace and resilience. By filling our minds with His truths and promises, we develop a spirit grounded in faith rather than fear. This renewed mindset transforms how we see the world and empowers us to live out God's purpose each day.

Chapter 3: Building Emotional Resilience Through the Word

Opening Reflection:

Life's challenges can test our faith, but through God's word, we can find the strength and resilience needed to endure. The Bible offers countless examples of those who, through reliance on God, overcame seemingly insurmountable obstacles. By turning to scripture during difficult times, we develop a spiritual resilience that allows us to face adversity with hope and trust in God's faithfulness.

Scriptural Foundation:

James 1:2-4 provides a powerful perspective on trials and resilience:

"Consider it pure joy, my brothers and sisters, whenever you face trials of many kinds, because you know that the testing of your faith produces perseverance. Let perseverance finish its work so that you may be mature and complete, not lacking anything."

This verse encourages us to see challenges as opportunities for growth. God uses trials to strengthen our faith, helping us build endurance and maturity.

Drawing Strength from God's Promises:

When we face hardships, it's natural to feel overwhelmed, but

God promises to be with us. **Isaiah 41:10** is a comforting reminder of His presence and support:

"So do not fear, for I am with you; do not be dismayed, for I am your God. I will strengthen you and help you; I will uphold you with my righteous right hand."

This verse reassures us that we don't have to face our struggles alone. God is our strength, lifting us up and helping us move forward, no matter the obstacle.

Life Experience:

During one of the most challenging periods of my life, I found myself clinging to Isaiah 41:10. It was a verse I read over and over, letting its truth sink into my heart. As I navigated my struggles, I prayed and reminded myself that God was upholding me. This experience taught me that resilience is not about relying on my strength but about leaning on God's promises and allowing Him to carry me through.

Practical Steps for Building Resilience:

Scripture is our guide to perseverance and emotional strength. **Philippians 4:6-7** encourages us to turn to God in times of worry:

"Do not be anxious about anything, but in every situation, by prayer and petition, with thanksgiving, present your requests to God. And the peace of God, which transcends all understanding, will guard your hearts and your

minds in Christ Jesus."

Through prayer, we bring our fears and concerns to God, allowing His peace to fill us and strengthen us from within.

Exercise for Resilience-Building through Prayer and Scripture:

1. **Identify Your Source of Strength**: When faced with a challenge, turn to a scripture that reminds you of God's faithfulness. Write it down, memorize it, and repeat it in times of need.

2. **Practice Gratitude in Prayer**: Take a moment each day to thank God for something in your life, even during difficult times. This helps shift your focus from fear to trust.

3. **Journal Your Journey**: At the end of each week, write down moments where you felt God's strength and peace. Reflect on how His word has impacted your resilience.

Conclusion of Chapter 3:

Emotional resilience isn't about facing trials alone; it's about finding strength in God's promises. By rooting ourselves in His word and trusting Him, we can endure hardship with peace and confidence, knowing that He is working in us and through us. As we grow in resilience, we become living testimonies of His grace and strength.

Chapter 4: Living Out Faith – Gratitude, Generosity, and Purpose

Opening Reflection:

Living a life of faith isn't just about what we believe—it's about how we live. The Bible calls us to show our faith through gratitude, generosity, and a purposeful life that reflects God's love and grace. As we let our actions align with His word, we become a source of light and encouragement to others, glorifying God in all we do.

Scriptural Foundation on Gratitude:

The Bible encourages us to embrace gratitude in all circumstances. **1 Thessalonians 5:18** reminds us:

"Give thanks in all circumstances; for this is God's will for you in Christ Jesus."

Gratitude is a powerful practice that shifts our focus from our struggles to God's faithfulness, allowing us to see His blessings even in difficult times.

Life Experience in Gratitude:

There was a time when I faced a period of uncertainty, and gratitude felt challenging. But by focusing on small blessings each day, I found myself more grounded in God's presence and less weighed down by worry. I realized that gratitude isn't about ignoring difficulties but about recognizing God's hand in our lives, no matter the season.

Scriptural Foundation on Generosity:

God calls us to give freely and joyfully. **2 Corinthians 9:7** says: *"Each of you should give what you have decided in your heart to give, not reluctantly or under compulsion, for God loves a cheerful giver."*

Generosity is more than just financial; it's about giving our time, love, and resources to serve others. When we give, we reflect God's character and open our hearts to His blessings.

Life Experience in Generosity:

One of the most impactful experiences in my life was when I volunteered my time to help those in need. Through these small acts of kindness, I felt a deep connection to God's purpose for me, and I realized how generosity blesses both the giver and the receiver. Giving, especially when done joyfully, brings us closer to God's heart.

Scriptural Foundation on Purpose:

Each of us is created with a unique purpose. **Jeremiah 29:11** reminds us of God's plan for our lives:

"For I know the plans I have for you," declares the Lord, "plans to prosper you and not to harm you, plans to give you hope and a future."

Embracing this purpose means trusting that God has placed us here for a reason, and by seeking His guidance, we find meaning and direction in all we do.

Living Purposefully Through Faith:

Living with purpose involves aligning our actions with God's will. **Proverbs 3:5-6** gives us a simple but powerful approach: *"Trust in the Lord with all your heart and lean not on your own understanding; in all your ways submit to him, and he will make your paths straight."*

When we rely on God and seek His guidance, our lives become purposeful, filled with direction and fulfillment.

Exercise for Living Out Faith:

1. **Daily Gratitude Practice**: Begin each day by thanking God for three specific blessings in your life. Reflect on how these blessings show His love and faithfulness.

2. **Acts of Generosity**: Find a way to give each week, whether it's your time, resources, or words of encouragement to someone in need.

3. **Prayer for Purpose**: Ask God to reveal His purpose for you, especially in areas where you feel uncertain. Reflect on scriptures like Jeremiah 29:11 and Proverbs 3:5-6 as you seek His guidance.

Conclusion of Chapter 4:

Living out our faith through gratitude, generosity, and purpose deepens our relationship with God and positively impacts those around us. By focusing on these virtues, we create a life that honors Him, allowing us to fulfill the unique purpose He has for each of us. As we continue this journey, let us remember that every act of faith, no matter how small, is a step closer to living the abundant life God has promised.

Chapter 5: Conclusion – Embracing God's Plan

Opening Reflection:

As we reach the end of this journey, we're reminded that personal transformation is not a single event but a lifelong process of growing closer to God, trusting His promises, and aligning our lives with His purpose. Every chapter in this journey of faith builds on the foundation of God's love, grace, and guidance, equipping us to face life's challenges with resilience and hope.

Scriptural Foundation for God's Plan:

God's promises are at the heart of our journey, assuring us that we are never alone. **Proverbs 16:9** reminds us:

"In their hearts humans plan their course, but the Lord establishes their steps."

While we may have our own plans and goals, it's God who ultimately directs our path. Embracing His plan means surrendering our desires, trusting that His purpose for us is greater than anything we could imagine.

Living with Faith and Trust in God's Timing:

In times of uncertainty, it's easy to feel anxious about the future. But God calls us to trust Him fully, even when we don't understand the full picture. **Romans 8:28** offers a powerful reminder:

"And we know that in all things God works for the good of those who love him, who have been called according to his purpose."

This verse teaches us that every experience, whether joyful or challenging, can be part of God's greater plan for our lives.

Life Experience of Trusting God's Path:

In my own journey, I've encountered moments where I didn't understand why certain doors were closed or challenges arose. But as I continued to place my trust in God, I saw how He used those moments to shape me, to grow my faith, and to lead me to places I hadn't anticipated. Each step reminded me of the importance of trusting in His timing and His purpose.

A Call to Faithful Living:

As we step forward, let us commit to living a life of purpose and faith, knowing that we are continually being shaped by God.

Proverbs 3:5-6 encapsulates this trust perfectly:

"Trust in the Lord with all your heart and lean not on your own understanding; in all your ways submit to him, and he will make your paths straight."

By surrendering our lives to God, we invite His guidance and assurance, knowing that He has a perfect plan for each of us.

Final Exercise: A Prayer of Surrender

Take a moment to reflect on God's purpose for your life and how He has shaped you through your experiences. Write a prayer of surrender, asking Him to lead you in the areas where you seek guidance and thanking Him for the journey of growth and resilience you've undertaken.

- *Example:* "Lord, I trust in Your purpose for my life. I surrender my plans to You, knowing that Your wisdom is greater than mine. Guide me each day and help me to live out Your will with joy, resilience, and gratitude. Amen."

Closing Thought:

Transformation is a journey that unfolds one step at a time. By embracing God's word, seeking His guidance, and trusting in His promises, we become a living testament to His faithfulness. As we continue forward, may we find strength in His love, peace in His presence, and purpose in His promises.

Epilogue: A Life Held by God

My life has been a journey of transformation, one marked by both trials and the grace that sustains me. Reflecting back, I see how God has shaped me through every season, each filled with challenges and growth. As a mother of six and a grandmother, I've experienced the deep joys and the heartaches that come with raising a family. I faced my hardest battles—like the end of my marriage—with God as my constant support. Through it all, He was my rock and my comfort.

Leaving California to start anew in Atlanta, and then moving again to Florida, each transition was a step of faith. Now, as I embrace this season of life, I find myself in a quiet place—a single life, an empty nest. It's just me and God. In this solitude, I feel His presence more intimately than ever. It's here I find peace, knowing He has always been my provider and promise-keeper.

Through the scriptures, I've come to understand resilience, gratitude, and the strength of faith. **Philippians 4:13** reassures me, *"I can do all things through Christ who strengthens me."* When I could have lost my mind to pain, He kept my mind secure. Just as He promised in **Deuteronomy 31:6**, God has never left me nor forsaken me.

This book, *Mind Spirit Science*, is a testament to that journey. It's an epilogue to *Be Still*, a continuation of faith, resilience, and hope. Even in moments when I thought I had lost everything, God showed up, healing wounds I never thought would close. As I look forward, I do so with the assurance that God has a purpose for me, and I embrace whatever He has in store. In Him, I find my identity, my purpose, and my peace.

Made in the USA
Columbia, SC
22 November 2024

46984385R00015

CHAPTER 20

The Crime Scene

J ACK TURNED HIS ATTENTION back to the crime scene. He glanced at Sadie, who stood nearby.

"Sadie," he called, holding out the glass, still wrapped in his handkerchief. "I need you to work your special skills on this. See if you can find any traces of what we're dealing with here."

Sadie stepped forward, ready to serve as a magical CSI unit. She accepted the glass with care, giving Jack a subtle nod of understanding.

Reaching into her purse, she pulled out what looked like a simple magnifying glass. To anyone else, it was a vintage piece with an ornate handle, but I knew it was something more.

With casual grace, she held the magnifying glass up to the rim of the glass, tilting it ever so slightly to catch the light. Her eyes narrowed as she examined the surface.

She moved her hand along the stem, running her thumb gently over its surface. "I'm checking for any residue or fingerprints." Her tone was casual. A quick glance my way, and I understood she was doing far more than that. I watched as her eyes shifted ever so slightly, focusing on something only she could see.

I caught a glimmer in the lens, just for a moment, like a wisp of smoke swirling beneath the glass. No one else would have noticed it, but to me, it was a clear sign that Sadie's magic was at work, disguised as a mundane inspection.

Sadie was in her element, using her subtle magic like a paranormal detective while maintaining the guise of a simple inspection.

CHAPTER 21

The Interrogation Begins

J ACK MOVED TO THE front of the auditorium, his eyes fixed on the trio. He gestured to the front row. "Come take a seat," he commanded, his voice cutting through the tense silence of the room.

Joanna hesitated, standing near the aisle with her hand trembling near her throat. Finally, she made her way up. Frances followed, her steps measured, taking a spot beside Joanna. A storm brewed behind her otherwise calm demeanor. Robert brought up the rear. He sat slightly apart from the women, closest to the aisle.

Jack stepped up onto the stage. He spotted two folding chairs in the wings and stationed them in front of the blank projection screen.

The theater's grand hall was empty now, and eerily silent. His voice echoed through the auditorium. "Let's get to the truth, shall we?"

I took a seat near the suspects. My eyes drifted back to Larry's body. Sadie had quietly covered it with a clean white tablecloth from the lobby, but the heavy aura of death was palpable. It was as though Larry's presence lingered, demanding answers.

Jack let the silence stretch, a tactic I knew he used to draw out nerves and anxiety. His eyes scanned the trio, finally settling on Joanna. "Joanna, why don't you start us off?" His voice was calm but unyielding.

She hesitated, glancing toward the stage as though it might swallow her whole. For a moment, she appeared frozen, her hand hovering near the pearls at her throat. Then, with a slow, deliberate motion, she smoothed her skirt and stepped forward. The clicking of her silver stiletto heels on the wooden floor resonated through the hall, each step louder than the last.

Jack gestured to the empty chair positioned at the front of the stage. Joanna perched on it, looking like a bird ready to take flight at the first sign of danger.

Jack allowed a beat of silence before speaking. "You were the director of tonight's event, the one overseeing the theater and its guests. Walk me through what you experienced tonight."

Joanna inhaled sharply, her fingers intertwining nervously in her lap. "It was like any other event," she began, though her voice wavered at the edges. "I made sure everything was running smoothly. Greeted guests, arranged refreshments. Larry was there, of course, mingling as he always does."

Jack's expression remained impassive. "As he always does," he echoed, his tone flat. "And how was he tonight?"

She avoided his gaze, staring at her hands. "He was Larry," she said simply, a hint of bitterness slipping through. "Charming to some, boastful to others. He brought his usual bottle of wine, you know, always needing to flaunt it." Her lips tightened, her eyes flicking momentarily toward the covered body. "He seemed on edge. More than usual."

Jack let her words hang in the air before responding. "On edge, you say. Did he mention anything specific to you? Any concerns?"

Joanna hesitated, her eyes darting briefly to Robert and Frances, who sat in the front row. "No. He didn't say anything outright. But he did seem a little different than usual."

"Different? How?"

She considered her answer, biting her bottom lip.

"He seemed jittery. He kept playing with that switchblade. I know it was part of his costume for the night, but it almost felt like he was planning something sinister behind the scenes."

CHAPTER 22

Frances Under Fire

JACK TURNED HIS ATTENTION toward the treasurer, who sat as rigid as a marble statue. "Frances," he called, his voice taking on a tone of command that left no room for argument. "Join us."

Frances adjusted her glasses, then clenched her jaw as she rose to her feet. She walked onto the stage with measured steps, holding her purse tightly against her side. There was a cold, almost defiant air about her, as if daring Jack to find fault in her. I noticed the way her fingers trembled slightly as she gripped the strap of her purse—tiny tremors betraying the calm she worked so hard to maintain.

Jack let her sit, allowing the silence to stretch just long enough to become uncomfortable. Frances met his gaze, her chin raised defiantly, though her eyes flickered with something deeper—fear, perhaps, or anger.

"Frances," Jack began, his tone level but probing. "How were things between you and Larry recently?"

She crossed her arms over her chest, eyes narrowing. "Strictly business," she replied curtly. "It's always been that way between us. Larry liked to push for extravagant spending, and I had to keep him in check. Last week, we argued over the budget for this event."

"Tell me about that argument," Jack said, his gaze unyielding.

Before Jack could press further, Robert leaned forward, his voice cutting through the air. "You don't have to answer that, Frances."

Jack raised an eyebrow, fixing Robert with a cold stare. "Are you serving as her attorney, counselor?"

Robert gave a slight shrug, his expression neutral. "Not necessarily. But we know our rights."

Jack's eyes narrowed. "Normal rules of evidence don't apply in every circumstance," he replied smoothly, not breaking eye contact. "So unless you're formally representing her, I suggest you remain silent and let me continue."

Frances cast a sideways glance at Robert, her mouth tightening into a thin line. Robert leaned back in his chair, crossing his arms but saying nothing more.

Jack turned his attention back to Frances, his gaze piercing. "Now, back to business. What was it you and Larry argued about?"

Frances folded her hands in her lap, her face a mask of serenity. "He wanted to dip into the theater's endowment fund. I disagreed."

Frances's lips tightened, and she cast a quick glance toward the covered body. "He wanted to throw money at marketing," she said flatly. "He thought it would draw in a bigger crowd. I disagreed. We have limited funds, as you know. It's my job to ensure we don't squander them on a one-night affair, particularly when other Halloween attractions could siphon our audience away."

As she spoke, I tried to reconcile this composed, dignified woman with the fierce anger she described. It was like watching a shadow pass over the sun. A sinking realization hit me: everyone had secrets. Everyone had motives. Anyone, given the right combination of circumstances, could cross a deadly line.

Jack nodded, considering her words. "And tonight? How did things unfold between you and Larry?"

She hesitated, a flicker of discomfort crossing her face. "We barely spoke," she answered, though her voice wavered slightly. "He was busy showing off."

I watched her closely, noting how her eyes kept drifting to Larry's body. Her fingers clutched her purse with a white-knuckled grip, as if holding onto more than just her belongings. Was she holding back the truth?

Jack leaned forward, pinning her in place with his gaze. "And what about his behavior tonight? Did you notice anything unusual?"

Frances shifted, her eyes darting briefly to Joanna before returning to Jack. "He was tipsy," she replied sharply. "Maybe more than usual. He was flaunting his wine and trying to flirt with young women, making sure everyone knew he had something special. Typical Larry."

Jack's face remained impassive, but I sensed his mind working behind those steely blue eyes. "You mentioned earlier that he was 'showing off.' For Joanna, perhaps?"

Frances's eyes flashed with something—resentment, jealousy?—before she quickly masked it. "He always had a way of worming into her life," she admitted, her voice tinged with bitterness. "They had history, and he knew how to play her. But it was a game I wanted no part of."

There it was—a crack in her icy demeanor. The mention of Joanna had drawn out a glimpse of her true feelings, though she'd quickly tucked them away. Jack didn't miss it either.

"Interesting," Jack murmured, stepping back slightly, giving Frances a moment to breathe. "Did you see anything tonight that struck you as out of the ordinary?"

She paused, her gaze dropping to her lap. "Only that he seemed agitated," she said finally, her voice subdued. "Like he was waiting for something to happen."

"Waiting for something?" Jack pressed, his eyes locking onto hers.

Frances nodded, her face pale under the spotlight. "Yes," she whispered. "He kept glancing around the room, watching people. I thought he was just in one of his moods, but now..." She trailed off, a shiver running through her shoulders.

Jack let the silence hang for a moment, then leaned forward. "Now?" he prompted quietly.

She took a shaky breath, her eyes haunted. "Now, I wonder if he knew," she said, her voice trembling. "If he knew that someone here meant to do him harm."

The room grew colder as her words settled into the air, like the echo of a distant bell tolling. I glanced at Jack, whose eyes were dark with thought. Frances's admission hung between us, heavy and foreboding. This was no simple disagreement or petty squabble. There were deeper currents at play, and I had a feeling we were only just beginning to wade into them.

CHAPTER 23

Sadie's Findings

SADIE CLEARED HER THROAT, signaling that she had something to say. In her hand, she clutched the wineglass wrapped in the handkerchief.

Jack turned to her. "What is it, Sadie?"

She took a deep breath, holding up the glass. "It's definitely poison," she confirmed, her voice steady despite the tension in the room. "I found traces of digitalis on the rim and in the wine itself."

Jack's eyes narrowed, focusing on the glass in Sadie's hand. "Digitalis," he repeated, his tone grim. "Foxglove."

Sadie nodded, shooting a glance toward Joanna, who sat stiffly in her chair. "It's a subtle poison," Sadie continued. "Tasteless in small amounts, but deadly. Whoever did this knew what they were doing."

I took a deep breath. "So, it wasn't just a random act. This was planned."

Sadie nodded, her eyes now locked on Joanna. "Whoever handled this glass had a deep understanding of herbs and their

101

effects," she added pointedly, leaving the implication hanging in the air.

Jack nodded thoughtfully. "Good work, Sadie. This confirms what I suspected." He turned his attention back to Joanna, whose face had turned an alarming shade of white.

CHAPTER 24

Robert Takes the Stand

J ACK TURNED HIS GAZE to Robert, who was fiddling with a
cocktail stirrer he'd plucked from his vest pocket. "Robert,"
Jack called out, his voice steady. "Your turn."

Robert's shoulders stiffened. With a casual shrug, he tucked
the stirrer back into his pocket and sauntered to the center of
the stage. As he sat, he spread his legs wide, elbows resting on
his knees, his posture commanding the space around him. He
adopted a relaxed stance, but I caught the way his jaw tightened,
betraying his feigned indifference.

"So," Robert began, a hint of challenge in his tone, "what do
you want to know?"

Jack raised an eyebrow, his expression impassive. "You were
the bartender tonight. Walk us through your interactions with
Larry."

Robert shifted his stance, eyes flicking to the side for a brief
second before locking back onto Jack. "Larry brought his own
bottle, as usual," he said coolly. "*Château d'Éclipse*, 2003. A Bordeaux he liked to show off."

He paused, a slight smirk curling his lips. "Not my taste, but you know Larry—always had to be in the spotlight."

Jack nodded, eyes narrowing slightly. "And what happened after that?"

"I opened the bottle for him, just as he wanted," Robert continued, his voice smooth but with an edge of irritation. His gaze swept the room, pausing briefly on Joanna before returning to Jack. "He was very insistent on pouring the first glass himself. He toasted with Joanna and a few others, making sure everyone noticed the vintage. Then he handed the bottle back to me to set aside. It stayed on the counter behind the bar for most of the night."

Jack kept his gaze fixed on Robert, his expression unreadable. "Did you notice anything unusual about the bottle or the way he interacted with others after that?"

Robert let out a short, dismissive laugh, though it sounded forced. "Unusual? Not particularly. But he was on edge. Kept showing off that ridiculous switchblade, like he was some sort of James Dean." His eyes flickered with a trace of annoyance. "Tried to hand it to me, said it was for luck. I didn't take him seriously. Larry was always playing the part of a suave gentleman, even when he was clearly off his game."

Jack allowed the silence to stretch, watching Robert closely. "This bottle of wine—where is it now?"

Robert glanced toward the lobby, his face tight. "Should still be behind the bar. I didn't touch it after he poured that first glass. Figured it was his business, not mine."

Jack nodded thoughtfully, his gaze unwavering. "Marley," he said, turning to me, "go to the lobby and grab that bottle. I want to take a closer look."

CHAPTER 25

A Ghostly Gasp

I NODDED AND MOVED toward the auditorium doors. The wine bottle was in the lobby, waiting.

But between me and that bottle was Larry's body, covered in a cloth, lying slumped in his seat.

I forced my feet forward, each step feeling like I was wading through ice-cold water.

A strange sensation washed over me—an unsettling prickling at the back of my neck. It was as though the air had thickened around me, charged with a strange energy. The hairs on my arms stood up, and I felt a chill creep up my spine. I glanced around, feeling my breath quicken.

That's when I saw it.

The air around Larry's body began to shimmer, like the way sunlight dances on the surface of water.

My breath hitched, and I froze, unable to tear my eyes away as something took shape—a faint mist curling upward, slow and reluctant, swirling in the dim light of the theater. I knew this sensation all too well. The room around me seemed to grow colder, the silence pressing in, amplifying the faintest creaks and groans of the building.

Larry's ghost was forming.

The mist twisted and thickened, unfurling into a familiar form. I watched in stunned silence as his face came into view—Larry, with his brow furrowed, his eyes wide and glassy, brimming with confusion. His mouth opened as if he were gasping for breath, yet no sound emerged. His arms materialized next, and in his grip was the switchblade he'd been brandishing all evening, reflecting the house lights in a ghostly, ethereal manner. It was no longer a weapon of bravado; it was a haunting reminder of his last moments.

A wave of nausea washed over me as I watched. Seeing Larry's ghost rise from his body was unlike any ghostly encounter I'd had before. This wasn't the gentle, lingering presence of a spirit from a century past. This was something new—the ghost of a murdered man, rising to a new, spectral existence. The shock of it pressed down on my chest like a weight, squeezing the breath out of me.

I had to force myself to look, to acknowledge what was happening. My mind raced, trying to process it. Someone here had killed him. Someone I had laughed with, chatted with, possibly even toasted with earlier tonight. A sense of betrayal twisted in my gut. How could I have missed the signs? Who among us was capable of this?

Larry's ghost staggered to a standing position, his eyes darting around in a frenzy. He looked down at his own body, lying limp and lifeless, then turned toward the stage, his mouth moving soundlessly. It was as if he were screaming, but no one could hear him. No one except me.

"No," he muttered, his voice faint and wavering like an echo in a vast cavern. "This can't be real." He reached out, his fingers trembling, trying to touch his own chest, but his hand passed through his covered form as though it were smoke. A look of horror twisted his features, and he recoiled.

He staggered past me, to the front row of the auditorium.

"Joanna?" he croaked, his voice cracking with desperation. "Can you hear me?"

He stepped closer to her, his movements frantic, waving a hand in front of her face. "Joanna!" His voice rose, edged with panic, but she remained still, eyes fixed on the stage, her face drained of color. It was as if he didn't exist to her.

"Why isn't anyone responding?" he stammered, turning on his heel, eyes wide as they scanned the room.

His gaze landed on me, locking onto my face with an intensity that sent a shiver down my spine. He stormed back up the aisle and pointed at me with the switchblade, his form wavering like a candle's flame in a breeze. "You," he snarled. "Tell me what's going on."

"Larry," I whispered, my mouth dry, heart thudding in my ears. "There's no easy way to say this, but you're dead."

His eyes widened in horror. He whipped around, staring at his own body. His face twisted in disbelief as he lifted the switchblade, staring at his reflection in its polished surface. His ghostly form began to waver, blurring around the edges, flickering like a weak signal.

"No. This doesn't make any sense!" His voice was a strangled whisper, laced with rising panic. He stumbled back, clutching the blade as if it could anchor him to reality. "Joanna!" he called again, rushing toward her. He reached out, his hands trembling, but they passed through her like mist. He staggered back, staring at his own hands in horror.

"You're dead, Larry." I forced the words out, every syllable feeling like a dagger to my own heart. "But I can see you. I can hear you. And I'm going to help you figure out what happened."

He stared at me, his eyes filled with a mixture of fear, anger, and confusion. For a moment, he looked ready to scream, to lash out at the cruel reality unfolding around him. Then he backed away, his body trembling. "No, no, no. This isn't real." His voice cracked, fading into a whisper as he began pacing, moving through chairs and shadows like a man searching for an exit in a room without doors.

I glanced toward the stage, where Jack was still questioning Robert. I caught his eye, and he immediately sensed my urgency. "Detective," I called out, my voice trembling despite my best efforts to stay calm, "we have a situation."

Jack approached, his eyes narrowing as he took in my expression. "What's going on?" His voice was low, controlled, but there was an edge of tension in it. He couldn't see Larry, but he could sense that something was wrong.

"Larry's here," I whispered, glancing at the ghost who had begun muttering Joanna's name again, his eyes glazed with hopelessness. "His spirit, I mean. He's confused.."

Jack's gaze hardened, and he gave a sharp nod. "Then let's make sure we figure this out," he said, his voice like steel. "Before things get even more complicated."

As I watched Larry's ghost pace, his form flickering like a flame in the wind, I felt a chill settle over the room. This wasn't just about solving a murder. This was about finding the truth for a man whose life had come to a sudden end... and that truth lay somewhere in the darkened corners of this haunted theater, waiting to be uncovered.

CHAPTER 26

To the Lobby

JACK NARROWED HIS EYES at the faint shimmer where Larry's ghost was standing. He couldn't see the spirit, but on some level, he could feel it.

"Marley," he said quietly, drawing me closer, "I need to keep moving forward with the questioning, but I want you and Sadie to head out to the lobby. Talk to Clara and Eleanor. They might have some insight into what's happening with Larry."

My heart skipped a beat. "You want us to leave you here?" I asked, glancing at the suspects, who were fidgeting in their seats, casting anxious glances around the theater.

Jack gave a tight nod. "Yes. I can handle things with those three. But if Larry's spirit is lingering, we need to know why and how to deal with it before this place becomes a full-blown paranormal circus."

At the whisper of her name, Sadie had stepped closer to listen in. She fidgeted with the pendant watch around her neck, and I noticed that the Roman numerals on its face glowed slightly. "All right," she said. "We'll see what Clara and Eleanor can make of it."

Jack glanced at the suspects, then turned back to us. "Go. And be quick about it."

Side by side, Sadie and I slipped out of the auditorium.

Clara and Eleanor stood near the concession counter, looking out at the street. They turned to face us as we entered, concern etched deeper into their expressions.

"Marley, Sadie, what's happening?" Gram asked. Her eyes flicked nervously toward the theater doors. The faint strains of muffled voices seeped through, adding a layer of foreboding to the lobby's eerie stillness.

I took a deep breath, trying to steady the whirlwind of emotions churning inside me. "It's Larry," I began, my voice barely above a whisper. "His ghost is walking around in there. I saw him rise from his body. He's confused and scared, and he doesn't understand what happened."

Gram's eyes widened for just a fraction of a second, betraying her surprise before she quickly regained her composure. "It's rare for spirits to manifest so quickly." Her brows furrowed. "Especially after a sudden death."

Sadie shifted beside me, clutching the pendant watch at her neck as if drawing strength from it. "Do you think Halloween has something to do with it?"

Gram nodded slowly, her gaze thoughtful as she scanned the darkened lobby. "Halloween is the one night when the veil between worlds is at its thinnest," she said. Her voice carried the weight of age-old wisdom. "It amplifies spiritual energy—and, unfortunately, dark forces as well."

"Are you saying he's a dark force?"

Eleanor quickly shook her head no. "Not at all—but there is unfinished business here. Strong emotions, particularly those surrounding a sudden, violent death, can tether a spirit to our realm."

I swallowed hard, glancing back at the theater doors. I could sense Larry's frantic presence just beyond them. "What do we do?"

Gram took my hand in hers. "What we *don't* do is panic. We need to understand his intent. Is he seeking justice, revenge, or simply answers? Until we know what holds him here, we can't help him move on."

CHAPTER 27

The Paranormals Prowl

GRANDMA CLARA AND ELEANOR exchanged a glance, and I followed their gaze toward the theater's glass doors. My breath caught.

Beyond the doors, on the sidewalk outside the Parthenon, a crowd of... well, *everything*, had gathered. The ordinary members of the audience had gone home, but an eerie parade of paranormals lingered under the glow of the streetlights, their forms shifting in and out of the shadows. My heart skipped a beat as I took in the scene. It was a supernatural roll call, and tonight, they had answered en masse.

A cluster of vampires lounged near the theater's entrance, their capes shimmering like liquid shadows. Their eyes gleamed like polished garnets, the pupils shifting between a predatory slant and an all-too-human gaze. One of them turned his head sharply, catching sight of me through the glass. He raised a hand in a gesture that was almost a wave, but it held the weight of something older, darker.

To the left, a group of witches stood in a huddled circle, their gowns of deep indigo and emerald green flowing as if caught in supernatural whirlwind. Moonlight glinted off their silver jewelry—amulets, rings, and bangles adorned with symbols I didn't dare decipher. Their whispers filled the air with a sound like rustling leaves.

Ghosts drifted back and forth, their edges blurring into the night like tendrils of mist. One specter passed right through a hydrant as he paced the sidewalk. Another hovered near the edge of the crowd, its translucent face fixed in an expression of longing or sorrow—I couldn't tell which.

The werewolves prowled at the outskirts, their hulking forms blending with the shadows. One of them turned its head, eyes gleaming like twin orbs of molten gold. Its fur rustled in the breeze, and I caught sight of a braided leather cord wrapped tightly around its forearm, glinting like a warning or perhaps a badge of rank. Its lip curled back, revealing a flash of sharp teeth, before it resumed its vigil.

Among them flitted the fae, their luminous skin casting an otherworldly glow. Their eyes glowed an unnatural blue, and their ears were sharp as daggers. They hovered at the edge of the crowd like restless moths, drawn to the theater's light yet wary of what lay within. One of them, a female with hair that glimmered like spun moonlight, turned her gaze on me, her lips curling into a knowing smile. It was unsettling, that smile—like she was privy to secrets hidden just beyond my reach.

It was a gathering of all the night's forgotten things, the paranormals in their true forms, come to see the outcome of this night when the veil between worlds had thinned to nearly nothing. It almost felt like a dream, an illusion conjured by the Halloween night. I blinked, half-expecting the scene to vanish like mist, but they remained.

Clara and Eleanor's dates stood near the theater's entrance, looking nothing like men out for a casual evening. One had his hands clasped behind his back, his eyes scanning the crowd, while the other gestured subtly, directing the flow of the milling paranormals. Their presence was calm but commanding, adding a layer of reassurance to the restless throng.

"They're not leaving," I murmured, my voice barely a whisper. I couldn't tear my eyes away from the haunting assembly on the sidewalk.

"No, they're not," Gram replied, her voice edged with concern. "They know something's wrong. They can feel the disturbance in the air."

Sadie stepped closer, her eyes narrowing as she studied the crowd. Her voice hushed with a mix of awe and trepidation. "It's rare to see so many of them all at once. They're drawn to the imbalance."

I swallowed hard, a lump of fear settling in my stomach. The paranormals weren't just here out of curiosity; they were here because they sensed the gravity of what had happened. Larry's death had stirred the supernatural waters, and now the creatures that usually lurked in the shadows had come to the surface, prowling, watching, waiting.

For what, I couldn't say. And that was what scared me most of all.

Grandma Clara turned to me, her eyes sharp, cutting through the dim light of the lobby like twin daggers. "Now that you've seen Larry's ghost, the situation is becoming clearer. We don't have much time."

Eleanor stepped forward, worry etched into the lines of her face. "If we don't help Larry's spirit move on before midnight," she said gravely, "he could be trapped here forever."

CHAPTER 28

The Restless Veil

S ERIOUSLY? I SHOOK MY head in disbelief. The thought of
Larry's confused ghost wandering these halls, his presence
lingering in every seat and shadow, was foreboding, to say the
least. I glanced through the glass doors at the gathering of paranormals outside. It felt like they were watching us, waiting to see
if we could set things right.

"Yes," Gram continued, her voice dropping to a hushed tone,
"but there's more." She paused, letting the weight of her words
settle like a fog around us. "It's also possible that if Jack doesn't
solve this case before midnight, Larry's ghost will get caught in
the restless veil."

The restless veil. The term washed over me like icy water. "I've
never heard of that. What is 'the restless veil?'"

Clara nodded slowly, her gaze steady. "When the boundary
between worlds is stretched this thin, souls can become entangled, like flies in a spider's web. The restless veil has been known
to pull restless spirits into its grasp. If Larry's death remains unre-

solved, his spirit could be trapped, confined, and unable to cross over or communicate with the living."

Eleanor leaned forward. "It's a terrible place, where lost souls wander aimlessly, forever trapped in their final moments. And tonight, midnight is the cutoff point. After that..."

"After that," Sadie interjected, her voice tight, "Larry would be doomed to haunt this theater. His spirit will drift through the seats and halls, replaying his final moments over and over, unable to find peace." She shook her head sadly. "It's not just a haunting; it's a kind of ghostly prison."

I swallowed hard. I didn't know Larry. What little I'd seen of him in life didn't impress me much. But the thought of his ghost, forever wandering the Parthenon, trapped in his confusion and fear, was too horrible to contemplate.

I glanced back at the auditorium door, where the murmur of voices drifted into the lobby. The clock on the wall ticked steadily, each second slipping away like grains of sand in an hourglass.

Clara continued, her voice now barely above a whisper. "And then there's the Reaper."

CHAPTER 29

The Reaper

I STIFFENED AT THE memory of the cloaked figure I'd seen earlier. "Do you mean the Grim Reaper?"

"Yes." Grandma Clara nodded solemnly. "He's waiting, biding his time. On Halloween, his role changes. Normally, the Reaper stands as a guide for spirits, ushering them to their rightful place. But if Larry hasn't found peace by midnight, the Reaper has no choice but to drag him into the restless veil."

My breath caught. The implications were staggering. "So, the Reaper would imprison him?"

"In a way," Eleanor replied, her voice quivering with unease. "It's more like being stuck between worlds. The restless veil is neither here nor there. It's a place of endless wandering, where spirits relive their last moments, unable to move forward or go back. It's a cruel fate."

Sadie, who had been quietly listening, crossed her arms. "And it's not just Larry's spirit that's at stake," she added grimly. "If he becomes bound to the Parthenon, this place will become a nexus for restless energy. We're talking ominous reflections in mirrors, cold drafts, whispers in the dark—classic haunting symptoms. The theater itself will be cursed."

The stakes were growing clearer with every word. If we didn't find justice for Larry by midnight, the Parthenon wouldn't just be haunted; it would become a magnet for dark forces, a place where shadows gathered and secrets festered.

Clara reached out and squeezed my arm. "This isn't just a murder mystery anymore, Marley. It's Larry's only chance to find peace. And the theater's only chance to remain a beacon of light instead of a vessel for darkness."

I glanced toward the auditorium doors, where Jack was questioning the suspects. He probably had no idea what was happening out here, what we were up against. We didn't just need to solve the murder; we needed to free a spirit from the clutches of something much darker.

"We're running out of time," I muttered, feeling the urgency seep into my bones. Midnight loomed like a dark specter on the horizon, ticking ever closer. "We have to figure this out—and fast."

CHAPTER 30

The Clock Ticks

OUTSIDE, THE PARANORMALS PROWLED, their eyes gleaming through the glass like stars scattered across the dark expanse. Inside, the heavy atmosphere pressed down on us, every breath thick and stale.

Sadie leaned against the concession counter, arms crossed, her gaze fixed on the floor, lost in deep thought. Clara perched on the edge of a plush velvet armchair, worry creasing her brow, while Eleanor stood near the glass doors, eyes scanning the supernatural crowd outside.

"We have to do something," I said. "We can't just leave it all to Jack. He needs more time to question the suspects and figure this out." My voice wavered, my heart thudding like a drum against my ribs.

Grandma Clara sighed, rubbing her temples. "I agree. The longer we wait, the stronger Larry's bond with this place becomes."

Sadie lifted her head, eyes narrowing as an idea flickered behind them. "We need to buy Jack some time."

We all looked at her as she took a seat near Grandma Clara.

Sadie continued, essentially thinking out loud. "There's a chance we could bend the rules," she said.

I stopped pacing, and I could practically see the wheels turning as the glimmer of an idea took shape. "How do you mean?"

Sadie gestured toward the auditorium doors, her eyes gleaming with a strange intensity. "Time is fluid on nights like this, especially in places like this theater. Halloween magic is at its peak. We could tap into that power to freeze time—slow it down within these walls. That would give Jack the chance he needs to solve the case."

Eleanor turned, her expression troubled. "Freezing time isn't just a simple parlor trick, Sadie. It's dangerous. It requires an immense amount of energy and focus." She took a deep breath, glancing back at the paranormals prowling just beyond the glass. "And there could be consequences."

Clara nodded, looking pensive. "True, but it might be our best option. If we create a bubble of time around the theater, everything outside will continue as usual. It's risky, but it might keep Larry's spirit from solidifying his bond here, at least for a while."

A flicker of hope sparked in my chest. "You really think we can do it?"

Sadie uncrossed her arms, her grip tightening around the wand at her waist. "We can, but we have to be careful. Time magic isn't something you dabble in lightly. It's not just about bending the rules; it's about rewriting them for a moment."

Eleanor stood. "That's exactly what worries me. Freezing time disrupts the natural order. It could draw attention from... things."

My stomach flipped. "What do you mean by 'things'?" I wasn't sure I wanted to know the answer.

Even though Sadie and I were the same age, she'd been raised in Salem, and she had been part of the magical community her whole life. "Ancient spirits," she replied. "Timekeepers. Entities that guard the balance between the worlds. They don't usually interfere with people like us, but if we mess with the flow of time on Halloween, when the veil is already thin..." She trailed off, letting the weight of her words settle around us like fog.

The October night seemed to seep through the glass doors. I wrapped my arms around myself, trying to block out the unease that wafted over us.

Clara stood, crossing over to me. She placed a firm hand on my shoulder, her eyes sharp and unyielding. "Marley, before we do this, you need to understand something," she said, her voice low and steady. "Anytime we meddle with time, they're watching. The guardians, the keepers of balance. They may not intervene right away, but they will notice."

A chill ran down my spine, and I glanced at the shadows stretching across the room. It was as if the theater itself was listening, waiting to see what we would do.

Eleanor sighed, rubbing her arms as she stared up at the theater's ornate ceiling. "And there's the building to consider. The Parthenon is old, steeped in history and residual magic. Freezing time here could amplify lingering energies, awaken dormant spirits, or even trap us within these walls if something goes wrong."

"Perfect," I muttered, rubbing my temples. "So we could end up stuck in a haunted theater with angry ghosts and ticked-off time entities. Just what we need."

Sadie let out a dry chuckle, though her eyes remained grave. "Essentially, yes. But the alternative is to let time keep marching on and let Larry get trapped here forever. We have to act now."

CHAPTER 31

Time Is Running Out

SILENCE DESCENDED OVER THE lobby, thick and oppressive. I glanced toward the auditorium doors, where Jack continued his questioning, every second ticking away in our battle against time.

Larry's ghost lingered in my mind's eye, a flickering, uncertain shape. If we didn't act soon, the natural flow of time would seal his fate.

Grandma Clara broke the silence. "If we're going to do this, we need to be on high alert. We'll create the bubble, but the moment we sense something from the other side, we cut it off."

Eleanor took a deep breath, squaring her shoulders. "And if it starts going wrong, we end the spell immediately. No heroics."

"Agreed," Sadie and I echoed in unison, our eyes locking in a silent pact. We were in this together, come what may.

"Then let's get into position," Gram said, eyes gleaming with determination. "We're stepping into uncharted territory, so keep your senses open. Anything could happen."

I was afraid, but also relieved. Taking action—any action—felt so much better than allowing fate to sweep us away.

"So, we create the bubble around the theater," I reiterated, focusing on the task at hand, " and time slows down for us, giving Jack the chance to finish his investigation."

"Exactly," Sadie confirmed, moving to the center of the lobby. "But once we start, there's no turning back. We'll have to accept whatever consequences come with it."

Eleanor glanced at Clara, who gave a tight nod. "Then we do this cautiously," Clara said, her voice laced with resolve. "We'll cast the spell and keep watch. If the guardians stir, we'll be ready."

Sadie lifted her wand, taking a deep breath. "All right," she said, her voice steady. "Let's freeze time."

I felt a ripple of magic pulse through the room, like a breath held in anticipation. I closed my eyes, bracing for what came next. Time itself seemed to shudder, bending to our will as the spell began to take hold.

"Here we go," Sadie whispered, her voice carrying a hint of both power and trepidation.

The air thickened, charged with an electric hum, as we prepared to step into the unknown.

CHAPTER 32

Stop the Clock

SADIE STOOD AT THE edge of the lobby, her wand raised, but hesitation flickered across her face.

"This isn't the kind of magic I would normally try," she admitted. "Freezing time in a single location is tricky—it's like trying to catch a gust of wind in a bottle."

Eleanor nodded in agreement. "We've all used the time portal in the shop, but that's different. The portal is anchored and stable. Here at the theater, we can't just wave our wands and force time to freeze at our command."

Grandma looked at me, then Sadie. "This sort of magic requires something tangible to grasp." She turned to Sadie, eyes narrowing thoughtfully. "Like your pendant."

Sadie frowned, her eyes drifting down to the silver watch hanging from the chain around her neck. For a moment, she stared at it as if seeing it for the first time, her brow furrowing. "Why do I have this?" she whispered, fingers grazing the cool metal surface.

I watched her, confused. "What do you mean? You bought it at the Wizards Market."

Sadie shook her head, eyes fixed on the watch. "I remember that now. But when I picked it up, it felt like it had always been mine. Like a gift from my grandmother." Her voice trembled, and she looked up at us, eyes wide. "Look: it's glowing."

Sure enough, twin beams of soft light emanated from its two faces, and a faint hum pulsed with energy.

As we watched, the faces of the watch began to tick, but not in the usual way. One of the faces moved forward, tracking time normally, while the other seemed to slow. "This is incredible," Sadie breathed. "It can monitor the flow of time both outside and inside the theater."

Clara stepped forward, eyes gleaming with a spark of under-standing. "This isn't a coincidence," she said, her voice tinged with awe. "This watch is a conduit to temporal magic, designed to help us manipulate the flow of time. It's a gift from the Other Side."

Sadie's eyes widened as she processed Clara's words, and she turned toward me. "Marley, your pendant could serve as a second anchor. It'll help us monitor and control the spell."

I looked down at my new watch. It, too, was glowing softly, its face reflecting the light from Sadie's pendant. "This is amazing," I stammered, staring at the intricate designs etched into its surface.

Clara gave me a knowing look. "I think this confirms that we're on the right path."

Eleanor moved beside us, her gaze fixed on the glowing pen-dants. "It's almost as if they were made for this purpose."

Sadie took a deep breath, tightening her grip on the pen-dant. "All right, then. We'll use the watches. We'll channel the spell through them to create a bubble around the theater. These watches will be our guide, showing us how much time has passed outside versus inside. And they'll warn us if we start to lose control."

Clara nodded, her face stern. "Remember, time magic is delicate. If these watches give us any warning signals, we stop immediately. No risks. Understood?"

"Understood," we echoed, feeling the gravity of the situation settle over us.

We formed a circle. Eleanor smoothed her skirt with an air of calm determination. Grandma Clara closed her eyes, inhaling deeply, drawing in the potent magic of the Halloween night. "This is high-stakes magic," she added. "If it starts to spiral out of control, we'll have to break the spell—no hesitation."

I glanced back through the glass doors at the gathering of paranormal creatures. Their eyes glowed in the shadows, intent on us, as if they could sense what we were about to do. Some raised their heads, nostrils flaring as they sniffed the air, while others remained eerily still, their gazes unblinking. It felt as if they were holding their breath, waiting.

"Ready?" Sadie asked.

"Ready," I replied, clutching my watch tightly.

Eleanor began moving her hands in slow, deliberate circles, tracing patterns through the air. "On my count," she said. "One... two... three."

The room grew heavy with energy, and the humming from the pendants filled the air, resonating like a low, ancient song. The glow from our pendants intensified, casting light across the walls like the shadows of moving clock hands.

CHAPTER 33

Time Stands Still

S ADIE CLOSED HER EYES and began to chant softly, her words flowing like water, weaving through the air. I felt a pull, as if the watches were drawing magic from the very atmosphere around us, anchoring it to the theater.

Time, stand still, the moment bind.☐
Stop the clock, while truth we find.

We all joined in, repeating the incantation like a chant. As our voices merged, the light from the pendants grew stronger.

The air thickened, shimmering with a faint glow. I watched as the room dimmed, the candlelit sconces flickering, their flames bending as though caught in a gentle breeze. A haze spread across the lobby floor, tendrils of mist curling up around our feet, swirling like miniature whirlwinds.

"Hold the energy steady," Sadie commanded, her voice now carrying a strange, echoing quality, as if it came from both within and outside the room at the same time.

Eleanor raised her arms, palms pressing outward as if against an invisible wall. "Time is a river, flowing and endless. We ask that its current be stilled," she intoned. Her voice grew stronger with each word.

Clara's eyes snapped open, glowing with inner light. "Let the theater become an island in the flow of time." Her tone was commanding. "Frozen, unchanging, until we release it."

A tremor ran through the building. The walls groaned in response, the air crackling with static. I watched in awe as the glass doors shimmered, a ripple passing through them like a stone dropped into water. The world beyond the lobby—the street, the sidewalk, the paranormals—blurred and slowed, as though someone had hit a cosmic pause button.

It worked. The theater now existed in a bubble, separated from the natural flow of time outside. It was as though we were caught in the eye of a storm, the world moving around us while we remained perfectly still.

Sadie opened her eyes, her face glowing with triumph and fear. "It's done. Time is frozen here, but it's still passing outside. We've created our bubble."

Eleanor shook out her hands, her eyes flicking toward the auditorium doors. "Jack has until we release the spell to find the killer."

Clara nodded, her expression somber. "We'll hold this temporal stasis as long as we can."

I glanced back through the glass. The paranormals were there, but from our perspective, they seemed to be moving in slow motion, a tableau of shadows and glowing eyes. It was eerie and mesmerizing all at once.

"We've bought some time, Larry," I whispered. "Now, let's catch your killer."

I turned toward the auditorium, then paused, remembering the wine bottle I'd been asked to retrieve. I used a napkin to pick it up, holding it tight as we returned to the scene of the crime.

CHAPTER 34

Truth Will Out

LARRY'S GHOST HOVERED NEAR the back of the auditorium, looking sad and confused.

Jack leaned against the stage, his figure sharply outlined by the theater's dim lighting. He was looking at Joanna, but she shifted in her seat, looking around the theater, avoiding his eyes. Her shoulders were tense.

"Joanna," Jack said, his voice smooth as honey yet edged with steel, "earlier, you mentioned that Larry seemed 'edgy' tonight. What did you mean by that?"

Standing beside me, Larry began to grumble. I set the wine bottle down and took a seat.

"Oh, here we go," Larry muttered, rolling his eyes. "As if she knows anything about my state of mind. Drama queen, as always."

I looked back at Joanna. She shifted uneasily, casting a glance toward Frances. "He had been difficult lately," she admitted, her voice strained. "Pressuring the board for more funding. He wanted to bring in bigger productions, modernize the Parthenon, make it more profitable."

Jack nodded. "And how did you feel about that?"

Joanna's lips pressed into a tight line. "It was reckless! The theater can't afford to cater to his whims. We've worked too hard to preserve its history. If we stretch our budget thin, we could lose everything."

"Oh, now she cares about preserving history," Larry muttered, pacing toward the stage. "Ask her about the time she wanted to replace the chandeliers with modern art. Nearly gave me a coronary."

I bit the inside of my cheek to keep from smiling.

Jack seemed to sense the resentment simmering beneath Joanna's words. "So, you disagreed with him," he pressed. "Strongly."

"Yes, but that doesn't mean I... I wouldn't..." Joanna stammered, her words trailing off.

"Oh, come on, Joanna. Spit it out!" Larry barked, waving a ghostly hand. "Tell him how you threatened to have me ousted from the board if I didn't back down."

I widened my eyes, surprised at the revelation. Jack couldn't hear Larry, of course, but the way he eyed Joanna suggested he sensed she was holding something back.

"What about tonight?" Jack asked, his tone deceptively casual. "Did you see anything unusual in the lobby?"

Joanna hesitated. "No. People were just mingling. Larry was showing off his bottle of wine, as usual. Chatting up Frances, trying to smooth things over with her, too."

"She makes it sound like I was groveling," Larry snorted, his ghostly form flickering with irritation. "I was merely explaining the financial benefits of my ideas. She wouldn't know profitability if it bit her."

"And how did Frances react to that?" Jack inquired, tilting his head slightly.

"She was polite," Joanna said, though there was a hint of satisfaction in her tone. "But you could tell she was annoyed. I overheard them arguing earlier this week."

Jack turned to Frances, who sat with an almost eerie calm. "Frances," he said sharply, "what was it you and Larry argued about?"

Frances folded her hands in her lap, her face a mask of serenity. "He wanted to dip into the theater's endowment fund. I objected."

Larry's ghost scoffed. "Objected? She practically bit my head off! Went on about 'safeguarding the legacy' like the theater's funds were stored in her personal vault."

"And why did you disagree?" Jack pressed, his eyes locked on her.

"Because it's irresponsible," Frances replied coolly. "The endowment is meant to preserve this place, not fund Larry's ambitions."

"Oh, here we go," Larry drawled, crossing his arms. "Her holier-than-thou routine. She was more worried about losing control than preserving anything."

I resisted the urge to nod in agreement. Frances did have a church-lady vibe.

Jack, meanwhile, let her words hang in the air. "So, he was angry. Enough to lash out?"

Frances gave a tight smile. "Yes, he could be vindictive when he didn't get his way. But that doesn't mean I poisoned his drink."

"Of course not," Larry sneered, drifting closer to her. "Because you'd never do something so crude. You'd prefer to dismantle someone's reputation, bit by bit. Death by a thousand cuts."

CHAPTER 35

The Bartender's Tale

JACK REMAINED NEUTRAL, HIS gaze shifting to Robert. "Robert, you poured drinks at the bar tonight. Did you notice anything unusual about Larry's wine?"

Robert crossed his arms. "Larry brought his own bottle, as he often did. I served it to him, same as always. Didn't see anyone tampering with it, if that's what you're asking."

"Except for the time you dropped that cork into my glass last month," Larry quipped, eyes gleaming with mischief. "Sure, you 'didn't notice' then, either."

Jack approached Robert, his eyes glinting under the dim light. "Were you aware of any tensions between Larry and the others?"

Robert snorted softly. "Of course. Anyone with eyes could see the drama unfolding between them. But that's theater people for you."

Robert's casual dismissal sent a shiver down my spine. "Theater people," he'd said, as though Larry's death was just another play. How could he be so indifferent? I studied his face, searching for any hint of remorse, fear, or concern. But there was nothing. Just a smooth mask of cool detachment.

A part of me wanted to grab him by the shoulders and shake him, to scream, "Don't you care that he's dead?" But I bit back the urge, reminding myself that Jack was in charge, and I was merely here to observe.

Still, Robert's nonchalance gnawed at me, leaving a bitter taste in my mouth. Was this a front? A carefully constructed act to hide his guilt? Or was he truly that disconnected?

The thought made my skin crawl. I didn't know which answer was worse: that he was pretending, or that he genuinely didn't care. Either way, I couldn't shake the feeling that Robert knew more than he let on. It made me wary, like I was walking through a minefield, uncertain of where the next danger lay.

Beside me, the ghost was grumbling again. "Oh, that's rich," Larry interjected. "Coming from the guy who staged a silent coup to oust the last director."

Near the stage, Robert continued, seemingly unfazed. "Still, that doesn't mean any of us had motive to kill him. If you ask me, Larry was his own worst enemy."

"You weren't exactly at the top of my friends list," Larry muttered.

Jack nodded, his expression thoughtful. "And yet," he said, his voice dropping to a chilling tone, "someone made sure he wouldn't be a problem anymore. The question remains: who, and how?"

I glanced over where Larry's ghost floated, arms crossed, an eyebrow arched as he watched the suspects squirm. Whatever had happened tonight, the truth was clawing its way to the surface, piece by piece.

"Joanna," Jack continued, eyes as sharp as a dagger, "did you see anyone approach Larry's wine bottle while you were mingling?"

She bit her lip before shaking her head. "No, but I wasn't keeping a close watch. I was greeting people in the lobby."

"Classic deflection," Larry muttered. "She was eyeing that bottle all night. Not that anyone noticed, of course."

Jack's eyes flickered, catching a nuance in Joanna's response. "Frances," he turned, "you were with Larry for a while. Did you notice anything unusual?"

Frances tilted her head, her expression cold. "Not really. He was his normal self. Gloating over the wine, flirting with guests."

"Flirting?" Jack's eyebrow arched. He glanced at Joanna, who bristled.

"Yes, flirting," Frances repeated icily. "He had a way of making everyone feel special—until they didn't. Like tonight. He was focused on impressing people, but there was an edge to him, like he was nervous."

Larry's ghost bristled with outrage. "Nervous? Earth to Frances, lady. I was as cool as a cucumber!"

Jack shifted his gaze to Robert. "Anything to add?"

Robert shrugged. "I saw Larry and Frances talking. Joanna giving them the evil eye. Standard around here. But no one touched the bottle after I poured it, as far as I know."

"And yet," Jack said, his voice cold as ice, "someone managed to introduce a deadly poison into his glass. The question is, who had the opportunity—and who had the motive?"

Silence settled over the room, thick with tension. Larry's ghost hovered, his eyes narrowed as he observed each suspect. "They all had motive," he whispered, his voice filled with an uncharacteristic seriousness. "And opportunity. But who had the nerve?"

This process was fascinating. I could literally see Jack piecing the puzzle together. The suspects were cracking, their stories unraveling. The truth was close, and Larry's ghost and I were here to see it all unfold. This wasn't just a performance—it was the last act in a deadly drama, and the curtain was about to fall.

Jack's voice echoed through the hushed theater as he circled around the suspects, his eyes sharp and assessing. Joanna sat stiffly, her hands clasped tightly in her lap. Robert was irritated, and Frances seemed to be deflating before my eyes.

The theater was cloaked in an eerie stillness, magnified by the temporal bubble that Gram, Eleanor, and Sadie had cast. I glanced at my pendant watch—still frozen at eleven. Time was technically standing still, but it felt like it was racing toward some inevitable conclusion. And there, just at the edge of my vision, Larry's ghost hovered, his form blurry and wavering in the ambient ligh, watching, listening, waiting for justice.

CHAPTER 36

A Deadly Glass

JACK CLEARED HIS THROAT, his voice cutting through the silence. "Let's talk specifically about the wine."

I watched their faces closely. Frances sat stiffly, arms crossed, her eyes fixed straight ahead, jaw set like granite. Robert raised an eyebrow, looking almost bemused, as though indulging a peculiar fantasy. But Joanna—Joanna's eyes flickered just a fraction too quickly. A tell. I filed it away for later.

"It was a Bordeaux, wasn't it?" Jack continued, his tone smooth and measured. "Larry's special bottle. Brought it in himself. Yet, by the time we got to intermission, he was dead. Poisoned."

I could almost see the gears turning in Joanna's mind. Her expression was a mask of forced calm, but the tension in her shoulders betrayed her. *Stay calm, I thought.* Let them react. *The truth will seep out.*

Robert broke the silence, shooting Jack a wry smile. "That bottle of wine was Larry's pride and joy. He wouldn't let just anyone near it."

"The killer didn't need to touch the bottle," Jack replied, his words hanging in the air like a dark omen. His eyes locked onto Joanna, sharp as a hawk's. "You only needed the glass."

"Oh, this ought to be good," Larry muttered, his ghostly form shimmering as he floated closer. "Let's see how she wriggles out of this one."

Joanna's eyes narrowed, defiance flaring in their depths. "You can't prove anything," she snapped, her voice edged with a hint of panic.

"Maybe not," Jack admitted, leaning back slightly, his gaze unyielding. "But we do know a few things about you, Joanna."

Jack paused, then turned toward the lobby. "It seems you have a knack for gardening. All the flowers in the theater tonight—they came from your garden, correct?"

Joanna forced a smile. "I do enjoy gardening. It's therapeutic," she replied, her voice taut.

Larry gave a derisive snort. "Therapeutic? More like obsessive. She used to lecture me on every plant in her garden. Oh, the tales I could tell about her prized foxgloves. She wouldn't let anyone near them."

I watched as Joanna shifted in her seat, her eyes flicking to the side for just a fraction of a second. It was almost imperceptible, but I caught it.

Jack crossed his arms, his expression one of calm scrutiny. "Therapeutic, you say? It takes a lot of knowledge to cultivate a master garden—especially when so many plants can be poisonous."

Joanna's eyes widened, her mouth opening slightly, as if to protest, but no words came out.

"You love your garden—beautiful flowers, exotic plants, some of them quite dangerous."

Jack gestured toward me. "Marley, you and I noticed some particularly striking blooms in the lobby tonight."

I stepped forward. "We did. They were impossible to miss."

"Foxglove," Jack said, letting the word echo through the room. "Gorgeous, but deadly. Few people realize that foxgloves contain digitalis—a potent poison that causes symptoms exactly like what we saw in Larry: bluish lips and a sudden collapse."

Joanna shook her head, denying his words.

"Digitalis purpurea," Jack continued, his voice as smooth as silk. "Foxglove, to the layman. Beautiful, deadly, and quite popular in ornamental gardening. A glass of wine, laced with just the right amount, would result in nearly instantaneous collapse."

Joanna's face turned ghostly pale, the color draining from her cheeks. I felt the air thicken around us, the tension coiling tighter. Out of the corner of my eye, I saw Larry's ghost drift closer, his expression keen and focused. He wasn't about to miss this.

"So," Jack pressed, his voice tightening like a vise around her, "you ground up foxglove leaves, maybe even distilled an extract. A few drops in the glass, and voilà—Larry's drink becomes a death sentence."

Joanna was crumbling, and Jack knew it. He had her cornered.

"That's absurd!" Joanna blurted out, her voice rising in desperation. "Do you really think I would kill Larry? Over what?"

Jack didn't miss a beat. His gaze softened, becoming almost gentle, yet unyielding. "Over your jealousy," he replied calmly. "You wanted more from Larry than a professional relationship.

But Larry flirted with everyone. You couldn't tolerate that, not when you wanted him all to yourself."

Joanna's face went white as a sheet. Her eyes darted to Frances, who stared back in horror, her mouth agape.

"I didn't mean for it to go this far," Joanna choked out, the truth clawing its way up her throat. "I just wanted him to slow down, to pay attention to me again."

Her gaze dropped to the floor, her hands twisting nervously in her lap. "I thought a few drops would make him feel sick, just enough to..."

"Teach him a lesson?" I finished for her, the bitterness in my mouth almost palpable. "Except you miscalculated, Joanna. Foxglove is far more potent than you realized."

Larry's ghost hovered beside her, his eyes narrowed in disapproval. "Quite the little mastermind, aren't you, Jo?" he muttered, his voice dripping with sarcasm. "Too bad you didn't bother to read up on dosage. A little too much, and—" He made a slicing gesture across his throat. "Whoops."

Larry floated just beside her, shaking his head in mock disappointment. "You always did have a flair for the dramatic, Jo. But poisoning me? That's low, even for you."

I paused to look at Joanna, her face drained of color. Could she really have done this? My mind raced, piecing together the fragments of evidence: Larry's boastful nature, his precious Bordeaux, the way Joanna had glared at him during the movie— and now this revelation about her gardening skills.

"No, it wasn't like that," she whimpered, her resolve crumbling. "I just wanted him to stop. He was always undermining me, always making me feel—"

"Small? Inadequate?" Larry interjected, floating closer. "Newsflash, Joanna, I had my flaws, but you chose this path. Not me."

Jack took a step closer, his eyes boring into Joanna. "You had access to Larry's wine. You know how to extract toxins from plants. And you knew exactly how to create a scenario that would mislead everyone into thinking his death was natural."

CHAPTER 37

Playing Defense

J OANNA'S EYES DARTED AROUND, wild with fear. "He was going to stab me!" she cried out, her voice rising in panic. "He pulled out his switchblade. I had to protect myself! It was self-defense!"

Larry's ghost burst into laughter, doubling over in midair. "Oh, that's rich!" he exclaimed. "Self-defense?

Jack crossed his arms, pinning Joanna with his gaze. "You expect us to believe that you feared for your life, so you carefully laced his wine with digitalis? Self-defense doesn't involve a premeditated act of poisoning, Joanna."

Jack stepped back, his eyes never leaving Joanna. "This wasn't a spur-of-the-moment reaction. It was calculated. You took the time to prepare the poison, waited for the right moment, and carried out your plan. This was no act of fear—it was an act of premeditated murder."

"No!" Joanna blurted out, finally breaking the silence. "You can't prove that! You can't possibly—"

"We don't have to," Jack interrupted, his voice dropping to a near whisper. "Not entirely, at least. But there is one thing that can reveal the truth. Marley?"

I blinked, taken aback. "What?"

"Check with Larry's ghost," Jack said, his eyes locking onto mine. "You've been watching him this whole time. Ask him what he thinks of Joanna's story."

Everyone turned to me in surprise, while Larry reared back his head and laughed. "Tell the detective that even if her claim of self-defense was valid, it falls apart when you know the facts."

"What facts?"

"My switchblade is a prop! Joanna knew that. We use it in theater productions all the time!"

I blinked, stunned at this new revelation. "Jack, wait," I interjected, feeling a sudden rush of adrenaline. "Larry's ghost just said his switchblade is a prop. It collapses on impact. It couldn't have been a real threat to her."

Jack's eyes narrowed as he turned back to Joanna, his tone icy. "You claim self-defense, Joanna? With a poisoned glass of wine? Because Larry pulled a theater prop on you?"

Joanna's face turned an alarming shade of red. "I didn't know!" she stammered, grasping at straws. "How was I supposed to tell it was a fake?"

"Nice try," Larry retorted, crossing his arms with a smirk. "You knew it was a collapsible prop. You were here when I borrowed it from the theater. You're just making excuses now."

Jack stepped back, allowing the weight of the moment to settle. "Joanna Elliott, you are responsible for the death of Larry Linwood," he announced, his voice cold and final. "And now, you will face the consequences of your actions."

Joanna's façade finally cracked. She crumbled forward, burying her face in her hands. "I didn't mean for it to go this far," she sobbed, her words muffled but unmistakable. "I just couldn't take it anymore."

Silence fell like a heavy curtain. Joanna's eyes darted around as if searching for an escape that didn't exist. Her mouth opened and closed as if she were grasping for something to say, some lie that could save her. But there was nothing. The truth hung in the air, undeniable and suffocating.

"You could have walked away, Joanna," Jack said, his voice unrelenting. "But you chose poison. You chose to take a life."

Joanna's sobs filled the theater, her confession spilling out like a flood. "I just wanted him to suffer," she choked out. "To know what it felt like to lose something important."

"Well, mission accomplished," Larry murmured.

His ghost was no longer wavering or aimlessly drifting. His form sharpened, his eyes burning with a cold intensity. Then, in a motion as clear as daylight, he bent down, face to face with his killer. "Did you really think you could get away with it, Jo?"

CHAPTER 38

Which Witch Is Which?

JACK STEPPED BACK, HIS sharp gaze still locked on Joanna. She slumped in her chair, the weight of her confession pressing down on her shoulders like a heavy shroud.

I moved closer, my eyes catching a glint of silver on her wrist—a thin, silver bracelet with a simple, delicate design. I looked more closely and noticed a charm in the shape of a figure eight: a lemniscate, the symbol of infinity, and a sign of timeless magic.

I looked down at my own wrist, where the forces of time had branded me with a similar mark. In the dim light, it glowed softly, an unsettling reminder of a visit I'd taken to the past. Along they way, I'd encountered three guardians of fate—and they'd warned me to be cautious with my powers.

"Jack," I whispered, nudging him and nodding toward the bracelet. His eyes flicked to it, his brows furrowing as he grasped its significance. A tense silence hung in the air, crackling with unspoken danger.

He turned back to Joanna, his eyes narrowing. "There's more to this, isn't there?" His voice held no accusation this time, just quiet, probing curiosity. "You're hiding something else."

Joanna's head snapped up, her gaze piercing and cold. For a split second, I glimpsed something ancient and dark swimming in her eyes—a flicker of raw, untamed power. Her lips twisted into a bitter smile, and she slowly, deliberately unfastened the bracelet, letting it fall to the floor with a soft clink that seemed to echo through the theater.

I felt the energy shift, a pressure building in the air, as if reality itself was warping around her.

"You're not the only one in this room with secrets, Jack."

Her voice was suddenly cool and detached. The air around her shimmered, like heat waves rising off sun-baked pavement. A low hum filled the room, deep and ominous, as a surge of energy crackled and sparked through the air. My skin prickled with goosebumps, and the hairs on my arms stood on end.

I watched in horror as Joanna transformed before our eyes. Gone was the composed theater director. In her place stood a woman who radiated an aura of raw magic, her eyes gleaming with a sinister light.

The shadows around her thickened, writhing like living tendrils, and the room filled with a pungent, intoxicating scent—foxglove, rosemary, and something older, wilder, like the earth after a lightning storm.

"She's a witch," I breathed, my voice trembling with a mixture of awe and terror. The magic pulsed through the room like a heartbeat, each throb making the air feel heavier, harder to breathe.

Jack took a step back, his jaw tightening. "*Daggers and Disguises*, indeed."

Joanna laughed, a harsh, brittle sound that cut through the heavy air like the crack of shattered glass. "You're clever, Jack. But did you think I'd let Larry make a fool of me without consequence? I have power. Real power."

She lifted her arms, and suddenly, the entire theater felt like it was being squeezed by an invisible fist. A wave of energy rolled off her, pressing against my chest, filling the room with the sharp, metallic tang of blood and earth. The lights overhead flickered and dimmed, casting eerie shadows that danced along the walls like specters.

"She's drawing on the theater's magic!" I cried, stumbling back as the ground beneath my feet seemed to tilt.

"Exactly," Joanna sneered, her voice echoing unnaturally as if it came from all corners of the room. "This place is saturated with centuries of emotion, of dreams and despair. I'm merely tapping into that power. You have no idea what I'm capable of."

My mouth went dry. She was even more dangerous than we had imagined. She had been hiding behind her mundane life, using her magic in secret—until now. Her restraint had shattered, unleashing something terrible and ancient.

"Magic doesn't justify murder!" I shouted, trying to steady my trembling hands. "You know that!"

Joanna's eyes snapped to mine, burning with fury and more than a hint of madness. "Maybe not," she admitted, her voice dropping to a chilling whisper. "But betrayal warps your sense of right and wrong until crossing lines becomes easy."

Jack stepped forward, his face a mask of grim resolve. "Save your justifications, Joanna. This isn't about what you felt; it's about what you did. You used your powers for evil."

Joanna's lips curled into a snarl, her hands balling into fists. "You don't understand!" she screamed, and the force of her voice rippled through the room like a shockwave, rattling the seats and sending the hanging lights swaying overhead. "Larry was going to leave me!"

Larry's ghost looked around, dazed and confused. "Leave you? We were never really together."

The air grew colder, frost creeping across the floor in intricate, twisting patterns. A gust of wind rushed through the theater, stirring the curtains onstage into a frantic dance.

I struggled to keep my footing as the ground beneath us seemed to tremble with her rage. I glanced at Jack, who was already closing the distance between them, his expression hardening with each step.

He stopped just in front of Joanna, standing tall, his voice like steel. "You know what happens now," he said quietly, his words hanging in the icy air like a death sentence.

For a moment, Joanna's eyes softened, the wild energy in them flickering like a dying flame. She glanced down at the bracelet lying on the floor, then back up at us, her expression eerily calm. "Yes," she breathed. "I know."

And then she attacked.

CHAPTER 39

A Witch's Wrath

FASTER THAN THOUGHT, SHE thrust her hands forward, and a searing bolt of light shot from her fingertips, aimed directly at Jack. He leaped to the side, narrowly avoiding the strike that left a scorched mark on the floor where he had been standing.

"Joanna, stop!" I yelled, panic clawing at my throat. But she wasn't listening. Her eyes glowed with a feverish intensity as she turned her gaze on me.

"You think you can judge me?" she spat, her voice distorted and echoing. "You meddle with time itself, Marley. You're like a drunk driver on the highway of history."

She flung her hand in my direction, and I felt a force like a hammer slam into my chest, sending me sprawling to the ground. Pain shot through my ribs, and for a moment, stars danced in my vision.

I staggered to my feet, my breath coming in ragged gasps, as she stalked toward me, her silhouette blurring and shifting in the flickering light. "You don't know what you're dealing with," she hissed, raising her hands again, dark tendrils of energy curling around her fingers like smoke. "You and Jack think you can stop me? You've only seen a fraction of my power!"

"Enough!" Jack's voice boomed, cutting through the chaos like a blade. He stepped forward, his eyes blazing with determination. "Joanna, this ends now!"

Joanna hesitated, the magic crackling at her fingertips faltering for a heartbeat. Then, with a snarl of defiance, she whipped around, unleashing another wave of energy that surged toward us like a crashing tide.

I braced myself, my heart pounding in my ears as the force hurtled toward us. There was no way to avoid it. And in that split second before impact, a single thought cut through the panic: This isn't over.

CHAPTER 40

A Phantom Army Rises

THE AIR CRACKLED WITH dark energy as Joanna hurled the wave of magic toward us. Shadows twisted and writhed like a monstrous tide, surging forward with a force that seemed to suck the light out of the room. The ground shuddered, and the theater itself groaned, on the verge of collapse.

I raised my arms, feeling the surge of power inside me. The walls trembled, the ceiling shook, and the lights flickered overhead as if caught in a storm.

My pulse quickened, and I thrust my senses outward, pushing through the barriers of time, reaching out with every fiber of my being.

I took a deep, shuddering breath and closed my eyes, reaching inward to the strange, coiled power that lay within me, the power that had awakened with my Saturn Return. I focused on the flow of time around us, the way it ebbed and flowed like a river, bending and twisting through every object and every corner of this building. I reached into that flow and willed it to open, to unravel its secrets.

I could feel the temporal bubble that Gram, Eleanor, and Sadie had cast, holding time frozen in place. I pushed against it, forcing it to stretch, to allow passage for those who gave life to this place.

The room went unnervingly quiet, a breathless pause where all sound seemed to drop away, leaving a ringing in my ears. Then, from that silence, a murmur rose—soft and distant at first, growing louder like the rustle of fabric and footsteps in the corridor.

It swelled, and Joanna's eyes widened. "What are you doing?" she hissed, her voice edged with panic.

I opened my eyes, feeling a strange calm settle over me. "We're not alone," I replied, my voice steady, stronger than before. "And you're about to learn how outnumbered you ar."

The temperature in the room plummeted, and the air turned icy. Shadows recoiled, curling in on themselves. A gust of wind swept through the theater, and they came.

They surged through the theater doors, slipping through walls and the cracks in the ceiling like wisps of smoke. Ghosts—dozens, no, hundreds of them—poured into the auditorium. Some were faint and barely visible, mere whispers of their former selves. Others glowed with an eerie luminescence, faces and forms distinct as they glided into the room.

I saw a woman in a velvet opera cloak, her features sharp and regal, as if she had come straight from a grand Victorian drama. A troupe of dancers swirled in, their limbs moving in ethereal, fluid motions as if they were still performing a ballet from centuries past. A man in a top hat and tails gave a mocking bow, his eyes gleaming with an unsettling joy. The ghosts of actors, musicians, stagehands, and patrons crowded into the theater, their spectral forms filling every seat, every aisle.

The energy of the room shifted, growing thick with their presence. The air vibrated with whispers and faint laughter, the echoes of countless performances that had graced this theater over the decades.

Joanna staggered back, her eyes wide with horror. "No," she gasped, her voice barely a breath. "This can't be."

"This theater has been a haven for spirits for a century," I said, stepping forward, the ghosts rallying around me. "You thought you could harness its magic, but you underestimated the strength of those who still dwell here."

Joanna's face twisted with rage. She lifted her hands, dark tendrils spiraling up from her fingertips. "You think this will stop me?" she shrieked. "I'll banish them all!"

Joanna screamed in fury and thrust her arms outward, sending a blast of energy toward the ghosts. It passed through them like a gust of wind, scattering harmlessly against the walls. The ghosts didn't even flinch.

I took a deep breath and reached into the flow of time once more, feeling its currents sweep around me. I pushed against it, weaving my power through the ghosts, reinforcing their presence with the strength of every moment they had ever existed. They glowed brighter, their forms solidifying as they advanced on Joanna.

The woman in the opera cloak stepped forward, her gaze locking onto Joanna. "You have no power over us," she intoned, her voice echoing with an ethereal resonance. "We are beyond time, beyond space, beyond the earth and sky and forces of nature. We are beyond your magic."

The lights flickered, and the theater trembled as I extended my hands, weaving my power through the ghosts. They glowed brighter, forms solidifying, advancing on Joanna.

"No!" Joanna shrieked, stumbling back. The ground beneath her feet rippled, the shadows recoiling like a retreating tide. Her eyes darted around wildly as the ghosts closed in, surrounding her. "You can't do this! I have power!"

"Yes, but not this power," I said, my voice calm and unyielding. "You're bound by nature. I'm bound by time. And they—" I gestured to the ghosts, who now loomed over her, "—they belong to neither."

The man in the top hat tipped his hat to me before turning to Joanna, his smile cold. "The theater doesn't belong to you," he said, his voice a chilling whisper. "It belongs to all who have passed through its doors, in life and in death."

Joanna's mouth opened, a strangled sound escaping as the ghosts pressed closer. The air around her warped and bent. seal around her.

Joanna's mouth opened, a strangled sound escaping her throat as the ghosts pressed closer, their presence sapping the strength from her limbs. I felt the currents of time swirl around us, tightening like a net. With a final surge of will, I thrust my arms forward, commanding the flow of time to seal Joanna within its grasp.

CHAPTER 41

Bound by Tradition

THE THEATER DOORS BURST open, and Clara, Sadie, and Eleanor rushed in. Clara led the way, her presence commanding as she strode forward, eyes locked on Joanna. In her hands, she held a coiled bundle of shimmering, enchanted rope, each strand pulsing with a soft, blue light that seemed to dance and ripple like liquid moonlight.

"Joanna Elliott," Clara's voice rang out, clear and unyielding, echoing through the cavernous theater. "By the authority of the Council of Guardians of Enchanted Springs, we are here to bind you and strip you of your magic."

Joanna's eyes blazed with defiance, her face twisting with fury. She raised her arms, magic crackling at her fingertips, ready to unleash another wave of power. But before she could utter a word, the ghosts surged forward, their forms solidifying into a shimmering, ethereal wall around her. Joanna stumbled, gasping, as her magic collided with the spectral barrier, fizzling out like a dying spark.

Eleanor stepped forward, her expression stern yet weighted with sorrow. "You crossed a line, Joanna. This is the consequence."

Joanna thrashed wildly, her movements frantic and uncoordinated. The ghosts held firm, their presence chilling the air until frost crept across the floor, twisting into intricate patterns. The temperature dropped further, biting at my skin as the spirits tightened their grip around her.

Clara raised the glowing rope high, her gaze resolute, every inch the leader of the Council. "You've lost your way, Joanna. It's time to atone."

With a swift motion, she cast the rope toward Joanna. It flew through the air like a lasso, uncoiling as it moved, a streak of blue light against the darkened theater. The rope wrapped itself around Joanna's wrists and ankles, binding her in place. Joanna screamed, a sound that tore through the air, raw and filled with unfiltered agony. The rope tightened, its light intensifying into a brilliant flash that forced us all to shield our eyes.

Joanna crumpled to her knees, the bindings glowing like chains of pure energy. Her screams faded into silence as the final remnants of her magic drained away, leaving her panting and defeated. Her head hung low, hair falling like a curtain over her face, her chest rising and falling in ragged gasps.

Clara stepped closer, her face set in a grim mask of authority. "You will be taken into custody," she said, her voice both firm and unyielding. "You will be watched, and your powers will remain bound until you have proven you can wield them with honor."

Joanna lifted her head, her eyes hollow, the fire of defiance extinguished. "And if I never do?" she whispered, her voice barely more than a rasp.

Clara's gaze softened, just for a fleeting moment, a glimmer of compassion breaking through. "Then you'll remain bound," she replied. "But that choice is yours."

The ghosts around us began to applaud, a raucus, standing ovation. Then they faded, their forms dissolving into wisps of mist before melting into the shadows. As they retreated to the hidden corners of the theater, the oppressive weight in the air lifted. The chill ebbed, and warmth crept back into the room.

Clara, Sadie, and Eleanor moved forward, their expressions resolute. Clara raised a hand, her fingers tracing an intricate pattern in the air. A swirling vortex of light and shadow materialized beside Joanna, its edges crackling with energy.

"She will be transported to the holding realm of the Council," Clara explained, her voice echoing through the theater. "It's a place where magic cannot be wielded without the Council's permission—a safe location until her ultimate fate can be determined."

Joanna, still bound in the glowing ropes, was lifted effortlessly by an unseen force. She hung suspended in the air for a heartbeat, eyes wide with fear and resignation, before the vortex expanded, swallowing her in a whirl of light and darkness. In an instant, she vanished, leaving behind only a faint shimmer in the air.

The vortex collapsed in on itself, sealing the gateway to the other realm, leaving the theater in silence once more.

I let out a shaky breath, feeling exhaustion wash over me like a wave. My limbs felt heavy, my muscles weak from the effort of summoning the spirits.

I turned to Jack, who was watching me with wide, awe-filled eyes. His expression was a mix of fear, respect, and something else—an unspoken question.

"Marley," he breathed, his voice barely audible. "What just happened?"

I glanced around the now-empty theater, the lingering chill of the ghosts still palpable in the air. I swallowed, trying to steady my racing heart. "I called for help," I replied, my voice rough but steady. "And they answered."

A wave of relief washed over me. It was over. We had stopped her. But as I watched her, trembling and drained, an unexpected pang of sorrow settled in my chest.

I knew she had brought this on herself, that she had crossed lines that shouldn't be crossed. But she was still someone I had once admired, someone who had brought beauty and art to this town. Seeing her broken and bound, I couldn't help but feel a hollow ache where respect had once been.

Magic had power, and tonight, we had wielded it to enforce justice. But it came at a cost—trust shattered, lives altered, and a shadow cast over the theater that would linger long after we left.

As I turned away, I felt a heaviness settle over me. This wasn't just a victory. It was a reminder that in a world where magic could shape reality, there was always a price to pay. And tonight, we had paid it.

CHAPTER 42

An Uncertain Fate

LARRY'S GHOST STOOD AT the edge of the stage, his translucent form flickering in the dim light. He'd watched it all—the confrontation, the binding, the ghosts retreating back into the shadows. Now, his eyes, still wide with disbelief, shifted to me. His expression was almost childlike.

"What's going to happen to me?" he asked quietly, his voice echoing in the vast, empty space. The vulnerability in his tone made my chest tighten.

I opened my mouth, but no words came. What *was* going to happen to him? I had seen ghosts before, had watched them linger and fade, but I had never truly considered what lay beyond. Now, faced with Larry's question, I felt helpless. Here he was, standing on the threshold between life and whatever came next, and I had no answers for him.

The fear in his eyes struck me, hard. In life, he had been in control. Now, he was reduced to this—a confused, uncertain spirit grasping for something to hold onto. My heart twisted, and I bit my lip to keep the swell of emotions at bay. I wanted to tell him it would be all right, that there was something good waiting for him on the other side. But could I really make that promise?

I glanced at Jack, who stood nearby, his face set in an unreadable mask. Did he know? Did anyone? The reality of death, of what it left behind, settled over me like a cold shroud. And I realized that magic, for all its wonders, couldn't make this part any easier.

Before I could summon a response, a burst of laughter echoed from the shadows, brightening the room like sunlight piercing through a cloud. Violet floated in, practically dancing on air, her eyes sparkling with delight. She exuded a lively energy that instantly chased away the somber mood.

"Oh, Larry, you have no idea," she sang, sweeping across the stage in a glimmer of light. With a playful grin, she looped her arm through his, giving him a reassuring squeeze. "The party's just getting started!"

Larry blinked at her, a bewildered half-smile forming on his lips. "Party?" he stammered, looking from Violet to me, and then back to Violet. "You mean there's more?"

Violet's laugh bubbled up again, rich and full of mischief. "Oh, darling, you didn't think the Afterlife was all fluffy clouds and golden harps, did you?" She leaned in and grinned. "Because, trust me, it's anything but."

CHAPTER 43

Don't Fear the Reaper

A T THAT MOMENT, A low hum filled the air, like a distant train approaching. From the shadows at the rear of the auditorium, a figure emerged, tall and cloaked in black. The Grim Reaper. His movements were slow, deliberate, and I took a cautious step back, braced to make a run for it.

He reached a gloved hand up to draw back his hood. Instinctively, I braced for something skeletal, gnarled, and frightening. But when the hood fall down around his shoulders, my breath caught in my throat. I hate to say the Grim Reaper took my breath away, but close.

The man standing before us was devastatingly handsome.

His hair was thick and tousled, an unruly mane of midnight black that caught the light like moonbeams tangled in shadow. His features were sharp, like they had been chiseled from stone—high cheekbones and a strong jaw that tapered into a slight cleft at his chin. His skin was tan, almost luminescent, contrasting nicely with the rugged five o'clock shadow of his beard.

But it was his eyes that captivated me the most. Two orbs of cerulean blue, gleaming with an otherworldly light, flecked with molten gold like distant constellations. Amusement danced in their depths, warm and unnerving at the same time, as if he held secrets older than time itself.

He looked more like a movie star than the dark angel of death. His lips quirked into a half-smile, and he winked at me, the gesture startlingly charming.

Violet sauntered toward him. "Where've you been, doll?" she called, squeezing past everyone else with a grin that could light up the whole theater. Without hesitation, she threw an arm around his shoulders and smooched him loudly on the cheek.

The Reaper chuckled, the sound deep and rich. "Up in the balcony," he replied smoothly, his voice like velvet. "Enjoying the show. You know, I do love those old movies." He jerked his thumb toward Larry, who blinked at him, still stunned. "Plus technically, I have until 11:59 to bring this guy in."

Larry's mouth opened and closed, his eyes wide as saucers. "Wait, you're the Grim Reaper?" he managed to choke out, his voice trembling with shock.

"That's me," the Reaper replied with a nonchalant shrug. "But you can call me Grim—or Reap, whatever suits you." He looked Larry up and down. "And you, of course, are Larry, my main act for tonight."

I couldn't help but laugh, the absurdity of the situation breaking through the tension. "Why did you have to be so scary looking before?" I asked, raising an eyebrow at him.

The Reaper raised his hands in mock surrender, his smile broadening. "Hey, why couldn't you listen to Sadie? It's Halloween, Marley!" He gave a playful shrug, as if that explained everything. "Gotta lean in hard on theatrics on a night like this."

"Well, mission accomplished," I muttered, shaking my head in disbelief.

The Reaper shot me a roguish grin, then turned his attention back to Larry. "Let's go, bro," he said, tilting his head toward the auditorium doors. "It's showtime."

Larry hesitated, looking uncertain, his form flickering with a hint of anxiety. Violet linked elbows with him, pulling him closer. "Oh, Larry," she said gently, her eyes gleaming with excitement and mischief. "We're going to have so much fun. You have no idea what's waiting for you."

Larry's brow furrowed, his curiosity sparking through the fog of uncertainty. "Fun?" he echoed, almost in disbelief.

Violet nodded eagerly, practically bouncing on her toes. "Wait until you meet Noël Coward and Dorothy Parker! And don't even get me started on Charlie Chaplin—he's a riot at poker night." She gave Larry a conspiratorial wink. "The Afterlife's got a cast of characters you wouldn't believe."

Larry blinked, his gaze shifting to me, as if seeking one last piece of reassurance. I nodded, giving him a small, encouraging smile. "Go on," I said softly. "You've earned it."

A slow, hesitant smile spread across Larry's face. "I guess I have."

The Reaper clapped his hands together, his eyes sparkling with humor. "All right, then! Places, everyone." He turned on his heel, gesturing grandly toward the glowing auditorium doors.

Larry hesitated. "Wait," he stammered, looking to Violet, "do you think I can get my favorite wine in... well, wherever I'm going?"

Violet's eyes sparkled with mischief, and she let out a soft, musical laugh. "Oh, Larry, darling," she said, linking her arm through his, "you won't need it to feel good up there."

The Reaper grinned, chiming in with a wink, "But that doesn't mean we can't enjoy a glass with dinner."

With a flourish, the lobby doors swung open. A blinding white light spilled into the theater, filling every corner with a brilliance so pure it took my breath away. It blazed like a welcoming sun, inviting and warm.

Violet laughed and tugged Larry forward, glancing back at me with a wink. "See you back at the shop, doll!" she called, her laughter trailing after them like the tinkle of silver bells.

Together, Larry, Violet, and the Reaper stepped into the light. It engulfed them in its embrace, their forms glowing and merging with the radiance as they crossed the threshold. The sound of Larry's laughter echoed back, mingling with the soft hum of voices from the beyond.

The doors closed with a gentle click, and the light faded, leaving behind only the lingering warmth of their departure.

CHAPTER 44

Erasing the Evidence

F ROM THE CORNER OF my eye, I saw Robert and Frances still seated in the front row, stunned into silence, eyes wide with shock. They had seen everything.

I turned to Jack, my mind racing. "We can't let them remember this," I whispered urgently. "They're ordinary mortals. This is too much for them."

A clattering noise interrupted me, echoing from the lobby like a jumble of pots and pans being knocked over. I cocked my head, listening. I'd heard that sound before—but where?

The theater doors creaked open, and in shuffled the wild woman from the Wizards Market. She looked exactly as I had seen her last: hunched over, her tangled mane of white hair spilling out from beneath a floppy, oversized hat festooned with charms, feathers, and tiny brass clocks. She was wrapped in layers of patchwork shawls and scarves, each one more vibrant than the last, creating a chaotic swirl of color around her small frame. Trinkets and baubles dangled from her belt, clinking and chiming with every shuffling step. In one hand, she clutched a gnarled walking stick etched with symbols that glowed faintly as she dragged it along the floor.

"Well, well, well," she cackled, hobbling forward. "If it isn't the most clever coven in Enchanted Springs. Up to your neck in temporal trouble again, I see!" She surveyed the room with sharp, bright eyes that sparkled with mischief.

Clara and Eleanor's faces lit up with recognition. "Meredith!" Clara exclaimed, breaking into a grin. "It's been too long! What brings you to our little crisis?"

"Oh, you know," Meredith replied breezily, waving a hand. "The usual: cosmic disruptions, bending timelines, and a touch of theater magic. I just followed the phantasmagoric floodlights!" She cackled again, her laughter ringing out like the chime of distant bells.

Grandma stepped forward. "We do have a bit of a mess on our hands."

Meredith huffed, muttering something under her breath as she approached Larry's body. With a dramatic flourish, she reached into one of the many pockets sewn into her shawls and pulled out a small, ornate hourglass. Its sands glowed faintly, swirling as if caught in a storm, each grain of sand sparkling with potential.

"Let's rewind time for our dear Larry, shall we?" she said, holding the hourglass aloft. She approached his body and pulled back the sheet to peek at his face. "Ah, he looks like he's sleeping."

With a deft flick of her wrist, she began to tilt the hourglass sideways. The sands within reversed their flow, shimmering and swirling faster, sending a wave of light cascading through the room. A sound like wind rushing through leaves filled the air as the light enveloped Larry's body.

Slowly, the light wrapped around him like a cocoon, and I watched, spellbound, as his form grew hazy, edges blurring and flickering. The theater around us seemed to ripple, the very air warping as time rewound itself. I caught a flickering glimpse of the audience, everyone once again in their seats for the briefest moment. There was a whoosh of air as their horrified gasps were sucked back into silence, expressions smoothing into neutrality as time was gently reset.

As the sand in the hourglass trickled back into its original position, the glow faded. The room returned to normal, save for one critical change: Larry was gone. The spectacle of his death had been erased. All that remained was the faint scent of foxglove in the air, a lingering hint of the event that had been rewritten.

Meredith gave a satisfied nod, tucking the hourglass back into her pocket. "He's where he needs to be now," she said briskly. "A quiet passing in his sleep, like the stubborn old fool he was."

I swallowed. "What did you do?"

Meredith dusted off her hands. "I unraveled this timeline's version of events, darling. We can't undo his death. Magic has its limits. But I could give him a death that doesn't tear the fabric of this community. A peaceful end, in his bed, where he belongs." She paused, eyeing me sharply. "Not a trace of his murder remains—except for those of us who know how to look."

Meredith's gaze landed on Robert and Frances, who were staring at her, mouths agape. "Now, now," she muttered, squinting at them. "We can't have these two carrying tales out of here, can we?"

Meredith's eyes twinkled with mischief as she shuffled toward them. "Always cleaning up after these messes, aren't I?"

"Wait!" I blurted out, stepping forward. "What are you going to do?"

Meredith grinned, a flash of mischief in her eyes. "Just a little mind-sweeping, dear. They'll wake up in the morning thinking they had one too many glasses of wine, and that's about it."

Before I could protest, she raised her walking stick, which began to glow with a faint golden light. She waved it over Robert and Frances, and the light rippled out, washing over them like a gentle wave. They blinked, their eyes glazing over for a moment before settling into a dazed calm.

"There we go," Meredith said, satisfied. "They'll be right as rain by breakfast."

Robert blinked, looking around in confusion. "Did we fall asleep during the show?" he muttered, rubbing his temples.

Frances frowned, glancing at me with a distant, puzzled look. "I don't remember."

Jack stepped forward smoothly, his tone casual. "It's just the theater playing tricks, folks. Let's get you both home."

CHAPTER 45

A Timely Return

A S HE GUIDED THEM toward the exit, Meredith turned her sharp eyes on me.

She pointed a gnarled finger at the watch pendant still hanging around my neck. "Now, Marley," she drawled, her voice taking on a weighty tone. "I'm going to need that pendant back from you."

I held my hand protectively over the watch face. "But I paid you for it."

"Yes, and I'll put the money back on your card." Her expression was serious, all hints of humor gone. I hesitated, my fingers curling around the pendant, reluctant to let it go.

"Oh," I muttered, feeling a bit foolish. "Okay."

I reached up, fumbling to unclasp it. Meredith cackled, snatching the pendant out of my hand with surprising speed. She pocketed the pendant, then gave me a wink. "Don't worry. I'll make sure you're fully reimbursed."

Next to me, Sadie mirrored my motion, reaching for her own pendant. "Do I need to return mine, too?"

Meredith's eyes glinted with amusement. She shook her head. "No, dear. You keep yours. You're going to need it." She winked at Sadie, who froze, her hand dropping away from the pendant in surprise.

Sadie blinked. "What do you mean?"

Meredith laughed, a sound both mysterious and knowing. "You'll find out soon enough."

Then, with a satisfied nod, Meredith turned her gaze back to me. "All right, then! Enough dilly-dallying. I have other timelines to attend to."

She shot a glance at Clara and Eleanor. "Let's catch up soon, darlings. We've got a few years' worth of gossip to cover."

Clara chuckled. "You know where to find us, Meredith."

CHAPTER 46

A Semblance of Normality

As the old witch shuffled toward the theater doors, her charms jingling like tiny bells in the sudden quiet, we all exchanged glances—Clara, Eleanor, Sadie, and I—and fell in step behind her.

As we crossed the threshold into the lobby, I felt a twinge of finality, like the closing of a storybook chapter. The heavy doors creaked shut behind us with a resounding thud, sealing the theater in its temporary stillness.

We accompanied Meredith through the lobby and out into the street, where the cool night air greeted us. The sky overhead was a deep indigo, dotted with countless stars that twinkled against the velvet backdrop.

The faint glow of the streetlamps illuminated the crowd gathering outside—the paranormals of every kind, their true natures revealed in the dim light. Witches in pointed hats, vampires with eyes gleaming like rubies, werewolves lingering at the edges, their fur glinting under the moonlight, and ghosts drifting like silver mist in the spaces between.

179

Across the street, a woman with silvery hair floated a few inches above the cobblestones, her shimmering gown rustling as though caught in an unfelt breeze. She looked ethereal, her gaze piercing and ancient as she surveyed the scene around her. Beside her, a trio of ghostly figures whispered amongst themselves, their words a series of faint echoes that reverberated through the air. It was like listening to a melody from another world, the kind that slips away just as you try to grasp it.

To our left, a cluster of vampires huddled near the theater's entrance, their forms sleek and imposing. One of them—a man in a fitted black suit that gleamed like oil—flicked an imaginary speck of dust off his shoulder, his every movement smooth and calculated. "Quite the spectacle in there tonight," he drawled to his companion, a pale woman whose lips were stained a rich, blood-red hue. She gave a slow, deliberate smile, revealing teeth that glinted too sharply to belong to anything human. Her eyes shimmered under the streetlamp, watching everything with a hungry curiosity.

Closer to the curb, a group of witches had formed a loose circle. They were of all ages: a crone in a tattered cloak, her gnarled hands tracing glowing symbols in the air; a younger witch with inky black hair spilling over her velvet robes, laughter bubbling from her lips as she conjured faint wisps of smoke into whimsical shapes. Around them, younger witches clapped and gasped in delight, their eyes sparkling with the thrill of magic. A burst of cackling laughter broke out, as if the very air around them had come alive with their joy and power.

Beside them, a lone werewolf stood silently, arms crossed over his broad chest. His hulking frame radiated strength, even in his human guise. His eyes flickered an amber hue, reflecting the streetlight as he scanned the crowd for potential trouble. A low growl rumbled from his throat when a nearby ghost drifted too close, his ears twitching to sounds imperceptible to the rest of us.

I caught movement above and glanced up to see a row of gargoyles perched along the theater's eaves, their stone-like wings stretched out wide, casting jagged shadows onto the street below. One of them shifted, the grating of stone on stone echoing faintly, and a cloud of dust sprinkled down, glinting like stars in the lamplight.

Near the marquee, a figure emerged from the shadows, his skin a deep, midnight blue that seemed to drink in the surrounding light. A djinn, unmistakable in his aura of ancient, otherworldly power. Smoke curled around his arms like serpents, and his eyes glowed an eerie gold as he studied me. "Quite a night for a murder mystery," he rumbled, his voice carrying a weight that settled into my bones.

I nodded, feeling a strange mix of fear and fascination. "You could say that," I managed to reply, my voice catching in my throat.

The djinn smirked, his eyes gleaming before he melded back into the shadows. A gust of wind swirled past, carrying with it the scent of spices and smoke, lingering in the cool air like a memory that refused to fade.

Not far off, a woman dressed in vintage clothing—complete with a delicate lace parasol—stood conversing with a shimmering wisp of light. Her voice was lilting, each word carefully enunciated as if she had just stepped out of an old-time radio broadcast. The wisp answered with a series of melodic chimes, musical notes that hung in the air before dissolving into the night. Their interaction felt otherworldly, a snapshot of a realm just out of reach.

Down the street, a banshee floated near a lamppost, her ragged form flickering in and out of sight like a flame struggling against a gust of wind. Her eyes glowed white, casting an unsettling light onto the pavement as she tilted her head back, emitting a low, keening wail. The sound reverberated through the air, sending a chill up my spine.

Nearby, a group of fae with delicate wings folded against their backs hissed in annoyance, their bodies shimmering before they flitted to a quieter corner.

Sadie moved closer, bumping shoulders with me. "You don't see this every day," she teased.

"No," I agreed. "This is a first for me."

We continued down the street, feeling the eyes of the paranormals on us—a collection of nods, smiles, and curious stares acknowledging our presence. A fae creature with silver eyes and pointed ears watched me with a knowing smirk before turning back to her companion, her laughter ringing out like wind chimes in a sudden breeze.

I took in the scene, my senses alive with the strange beauty and danger of it all. The paranormals, each with their stories, their unique brands of magic, had gathered here tonight. They belonged to the fabric of Enchanted Springs, woven into the cobblestones, the alleyways, and the air itself. And tonight, for just a few hours, they walked freely, revealing their true selves under the stars.

CHAPTER 47

The Bell Tolls

THEN, FROM THE COURTHOUSE rotunda, the clock began to chime. Time was flowing normally again, and we'd reached the midnight hour.

The first note rang out clear and deliberate, filling the night with an almost solemn finality. At the sound, a wave of magic rippled through the crowd, like a shiver passing over water. The paranormals froze, their forms wavering in the moonlight. I watched, breath caught in my throat, as they began to transform.

The vampires' crimson eyes dulled, fading into the ordinary browns and blues of the townsfolk. The witches' pointed hats and cloaks blurred, melting into scarves, jackets, and mundane hoods. The werewolf nearby stretched his arms, his eyes dimming to a warm brown as his posture softened into that of a weary man.

Above us, the gargoyles stiffened, their wings folding in as they solidified into stone statues, assuming their dormant, watchful positions on the theater's eaves.

In mere moments, the magical façade was back, leaving behind a crowd of ordinary people bathed in the glow of streetlamps. But the memory of their true forms lingered in the air, a reminder that tonight had been something extraordinary.

Meredith hobbled to a stop and turned to us, her charms jingling with each movement. "Ah, it's been quite the night, hasn't it?" She cackled, her eyes gleaming with mirth. "A proper Halloween, if I do say so myself!"

Across the street, a group of witches in their mundane forms laughed, their faces now those of familiar townsfolk—a librarian, a pharmacist, a waitress from the coffee shop. They glanced back at us, their eyes still sparkling with the residue of magic, before they headed down the street.

The ghosts, who had drifted at the edges of the gathering, vanished entirely, leaving behind only the faintest whisper in the breeze.

At the final stroke of midnight, a deep stillness settled over Enchanted Springs. The town had returned to normal, but I could still feel the pulse of magic thrumming beneath the surface. Tonight had been a fleeting glimpse into the hidden world that existed all around us.

Meredith watched this transformation with a satisfied nod. "Ah, there we go," she muttered. "The grand unmasking. Always a sight to see." She shot a glance at me, a smirk tugging at the corners of her mouth. "Don't look so shocked, dear. Midnight's the curfew for us all."

She sighed, a hint of wistfulness creeping into her voice. "Well, time waits for no one—not even a meddlesome old witch." She adjusted the trinkets on her belt, eyes scanning the dispersing crowd with a satisfied nod.

"You could always stay a bit longer," Eleanor offered, a hint of playfulness in her voice.

Meredith snorted. "Tempting, but no. I've got timelines to tend to, other messes to straighten out."

She paused, her gaze shifting to Sadie. "Remember what I said, dear. Keep that pendant close. You're going to need it."

Sadie nodded, her eyes wide, but a small, determined smile touched her lips. "I will."

"And as for you," Meredith said, turning her sharp gaze on me. She tapped her chin, eyes gleaming. "You've got potential. Don't waste it."

With that, she turned on her heel, her charms jingling merrily as she hobbled down the street. We watched her go until she rounded a corner and disappeared into the shadows, leaving behind a swirl of leaves caught in a sudden gust of wind.

"Well, looks like the party's over," Sadie murmured, tucking her pendant back under her shirt. "Everyone's heading home."

I nodded, the hint of a smile tugging at my lips. "Yeah. It's way past my bedtime."

Clara wrapped an arm around my shoulders, her warmth grounding me. "You did well tonight, Marley. You both did."

A flicker of movement caught my eye. From across the street, Clara and Eleanor's wizard dates approached.

"Ladies," one of the wizards said, offering a respectful nod, "it's been quite a night. Allow us to escort you home."

Clara and Eleanor exchanged amused, appreciative glances. "Well, it seems our gentlemen have arrived."

Grandma Clara turned to us. "Go home, girls. You've done more than enough tonight."

Eleanor nodded in agreement, her eyes softening as she looked at me. "I'll see you at the shop."

Clara and Eleanor linked arms with their escorts, who led them down the street, their footsteps echoing in the quiet. As they walked away, I couldn't help but notice the way the wizards subtly gestured, casting a final layer of protective magic around Sadie and me. The air shimmered briefly, then settled, leaving behind a sense of peace and safety.

Sadie let out a soft sigh. "That looks so romantic. I wonder if they have grandsons."

I looked up at the courthouse clock, its face glowing softly in the moonlight. Midnight had come and gone, and with it, the enchantment of the night had receded. Enchanted Springs had resumed its normal facade, but I knew the magic lingered beneath the surface, ready to awaken when the moment was right.